Mona? Moving away?

Ashleigh felt like the wind had been knocked from her. She gulped for air, but there wasn't enough to fill her lungs.

This was too cruel. Ashleigh still felt the loss of the yearlings. And with all the pain she had suffered at losing Shadow, this was too much! It was bad enough to miss the horses, but she couldn't lose her best friend. *She just couldn't!*

"When are you moving?" Ashleigh finally managed to speak a whole sentence.

Mona took a deep breath and choked back a sob. "I don't know. We're putting our house up for sale on Monday. My mother and I are going to stay here until the farm is sold, then we'll move to California with my dad. I'm going to miss you so much, Ash!"

Not live next to Mona? Ashleigh's mind reeled. What about all their plans? What about all the foals they were going to raise together and race?

"I can't believe this!" Ashleigh cried. "This isn't happening! What about the Halloween party in a couple of weeks? What about all the holidays that we were going to spend together? You can't leave!"

Collect all the books in the Ashleigh series:

Ashleigh #1: *Lightning's Last Hope*

Ashleigh #2: *A Horse for Christmas*

Ashleigh #3: *Waiting for Stardust*

Ashleigh #4: *Good-bye, Midnight Wanderer*

Ashleigh #5: *The Forbidden Stallion*

Ashleigh #6: *A Dangerous Ride*

Ashleigh #7: *Derby Day*

Ashleigh #8: *The Lost Foal*

Ashleigh #9: *Holiday Homecoming*

Ashleigh #10: *Derby Dreams**

ASHLEIGH'S Thoroughbred Collection

Star of Shadowbrook Farm

The Forgotten Filly

Battlecry Forever!

*Coming soon

THOROUGHBRED

Ashleigh

HOLIDAY HOMECOMING

CREATED BY
JOANNA CAMPBELL

WRITTEN BY
CHRIS PLATT

HarperEntertainment
An Imprint of HarperCollinsPublishers

HarperEntertainment
An Imprint of HarperCollins*Publishers*
10 East 53rd Street, New York, NY 10022–5299

This is a work of fiction. The characters, incidents, and dialogues are
products of the author's imagination and are not to be construed
as real. Any resemblance to actual events or persons,
living or dead, is entirely coincidental.

Produced by 17th Street Productions, Inc.,
an Alloy Online, Inc., company

ISBN 0-06-105876-9

HarperCollins®, 🔥®, and HarperEntertainment™ are trademarks of
HarperCollins Publishers Inc.

Cover art © 2000 by 17th Street Productions, Inc.,
an Alloy Online, Inc., company

First printing: November 2000

Printed in the United States of America

Visit HarperEntertainment on the World Wide Web at
www.harpercollins.com

❖ 10 9 8 7 6 5 4 3 2 1

For Kari & Jen, two very special friends

"Here, Shadow. Here, Go Gen," eleven-year-old Ashleigh Griffen called as she climbed the white-board fence that surrounded the broodmare paddock. She adjusted the lead rope and halter slung over her shoulder. "Time to head in."

She pulled herself over the top rail and paused. In the large, twenty-acre paddock, ten broodmares grazed peacefully. Their foals frolicked, napped, and nibbled tender shoots of grass. In the smaller, five-acre paddock, Edgardale's yearlings tested their strength and speed as they raced around the pasture, kicking up their heels and nipping at one another's flanks.

Ashleigh smiled. As usual Bandit, My Georgina's light bay colt, was in the lead and trying to stir up trouble. Ashleigh's smile faded a bit as she watched the beautiful yearlings circle the paddock with their manes and tails flying. This time of year was always bittersweet.

Prepping the yearlings for the annual Keeneland sale was a lot of fun. But at the sale's end, the yearlings would have new homes away from Edgardale. Ashleigh rarely saw them again.

The high-pitched whinny of a foal reminded Ashleigh that she had a job to do. Her mother had asked her to bring Go Gen and her filly, Shadow, into the barn.

"Come on, girls, you can move faster than that!" Ashleigh laughed as Go Gen lifted her head from the Kentucky bluegrass. The big gray mare casually headed in Ashleigh's direction. "I don't have all day, you know."

Ashleigh jumped to the ground, her sneakers making a soft thump as she hit the drying grass. She looked at the large oak and maple trees that dotted Edgardale's landscape. The leaves were turning beautiful shades of yellows, oranges, and reds. She closed her eyes and breathed deeply of the cool Kentucky air. Fall had definitely arrived.

Ashleigh's hazel eyes flew open at the sound of hoofbeats. She smiled as Shadow, a black filly with three white socks and a blaze, streaked across the paddock, challenging her mother to a race. Ashleigh thought she'd have to climb back onto the fence, but Shadow began to slow. The filly shifted her weight to her haunches as she came to a sliding stop three feet from where Ashleigh stood.

"You're such a show-off," Ashleigh said fondly as she ruffled Shadow's wispy black mane.

Ashleigh had been there when Shadow was born, and they had developed a bond. That bond had grown even stronger several months ago. Shadow had been stolen, and Ashleigh had been the only one who believed the filly was still alive. Ashleigh smiled. She was glad Shadow was only six months old. She would have the filly all to herself for a whole year before Shadow would be sold at auction.

Ashleigh giggled as Shadow nibbled at the lead rope and tried to insert her nose into the blue nylon halter. "No, silly, this is for your mother," she said. "You won't fit into it for at least another year." She pulled the halter over Go Gen's head and hooked the buckle, then led the horses toward the broodmare barn.

As they walked beside the fence, Ashleigh noticed how close Shadow walked to Go Gen's side. Ever since the filly had been stolen from Edgardale and was separated from her dam for many days, Shadow never strayed far from Go Gen's side. Tomorrow was weaning day at Edgardale. Ashleigh had a feeling it was going to be especially hard on Shadow.

They reached the gate, and Ashleigh unlatched it, leading Go Gen through the opening. Another gust of wind banged the gate closed. Ashleigh didn't notice that Shadow was left behind until she heard a frightened whinny and the sound of hoofbeats as the black filly raced frantically up and down the fence.

"Easy, Shadow," Ashleigh said as she turned Go Gen back toward the gate.

The big mare nickered to her foal and began to dance at the end of the lead rope. Ashleigh held on tight, pulling Go Gen toward the gate, but Shadow cantered in the opposite direction with a panicked whinny.

"Shadow, come here," Ashleigh called as she fought with Go Gen. The big gray mare tried to follow her foal up the fence line, but Ashleigh held on tight, digging her heels into the dirt as Go Gen tossed her head and called desperately to her foal.

"Ashleigh," Mr. Griffen hollered as he stepped from the barn. "What's going on?"

Ashleigh turned to her father, her heart pounding in her chest as Shadow pivoted on her haunches and raced back toward them. "Shadow got stuck on the other side of the fence," she cried. "She's scared, and she's running crazy." She winced as Go Gen tossed her head, jerking hard.

Derek Griffen dropped the bucket of feed he was carrying and ran toward his daughter. "Give me the mare, Ash." He grabbed for the lead rope and tried to calm the agitated broodmare. "Open the gate for Shadow before she decides to try to jump it or go through it."

Shadow turned and ran toward the gate as Ashleigh

approached. "Whoa," Ashleigh said as she waved her hands in the air, trying to discourage the filly from jumping. Ashleigh knew that Shadow was too little to clear the fence, but young horses often did things that got them into serious trouble.

Shadow skidded to a stop and bumped the gate with her small, delicately muscled chest, nickering desperately to her dam.

"Easy, girl," Ashleigh crooned. "I'm going to open it right now."

Shadow snorted, dancing on her little hooves as she tossed her finely shaped head. Ashleigh worked at the latch, but she was in too much of a hurry and missed it on her first attempt. As Go Gen whinnied once more, Shadow charged the fence, slinging her forelegs over the upper rail and struggling to pop over the top. Ashleigh slipped on the damp grass and fell backward.

Elaine Griffen ran from the barn, blond hair flying from under her hat as she sprinted to Ashleigh's side. "Caroline," she called to Ashleigh's older sister as she helped Ashleigh to her feet. "Take that mare from your father so he can help Shadow!"

"I'm all right, Mom," Ashleigh said as she stood and tested her shaky legs. She started forward to help the black filly, who now had her front legs stuck over the top rail and was crying out in fright.

"Stay here, Ashleigh," Mrs. Griffen warned. "I don't want you getting in the way of a flailing hoof when your father tries to set Shadow free."

"Mom, help!" Caroline called as the big gray mare dragged her forward, trying to reach her foal.

"I'll do it," Ashleigh said to her mother. "Dad needs you."

If the situation hadn't been dangerous, Ashleigh might have laughed. Poor Caroline was the only member of their family who didn't like horses. Although she helped with their family-run horse farm, thirteen-year-old Caroline wasn't very good with horses. Even their younger brother, Rory, was a bigger help than Caroline.

"Here, I've got her," Ashleigh said as she took the lead rope and pulled down sharply, drawing the mare's attention. "You go get Rory. He's standing up at the barn, looking scared to death. And get Jonas, too."

A moment later Jonas McIntyre, Edgardale's only hired hand, came running from the barn. Ashleigh had never seen the old groom move so fast.

"Jonas, help me get this filly's legs back over the fence," Mr. Griffen said as he worked quickly. "We're going to have to lift them a few inches more, then push her backward."

"Watch so Shadow doesn't hit you," Mrs. Griffen

warned as the filly began tossing her head and scrambling her legs along the top rail again.

Ashleigh sucked in her breath. Shadow's legs were so delicate, it wouldn't take much to snap them. Ashleigh's stomach flopped as she thought about the damage that could be done to those young tendons as they ground back and forth against the wood of the fence.

Ashleigh knew that if Shadow hurt herself badly at this young age, she might never get the chance to become a great racehorse like her full brother, Aladdin. Shadow's career as a racer would be over before it started. Ashleigh held her breath while Jonas and her father worked.

"Just a little bit more," Derek Griffen said to the stable hand. "Now, push her back!"

Ashleigh heaved a sigh of relief as her father and Jonas lifted the filly's legs clear of the fence. But as Shadow threw her weight backward, scrambling to be free, she began to tip.

"No!" Ashleigh cried as she watched the filly land on her back and flounder in the grass, her legs beating against the ground as she struggled to rise.

Go Gen snorted and lunged toward the fence, dragging Ashleigh with her, but Ashleigh didn't mind. She had the same goal as the gray mare's. She wanted to get to Shadow.

"Hurry and get that gate open," Mr. Griffen

instructed Jonas. "Ashleigh, give me that mare." He took the lead rope as the gate swung wide.

By now Shadow had gained her footing. She took several wavering steps before getting her balance and bolting out the gate in a wild panic. Ashleigh watched closely as the filly ran to her dam's side and began to nurse. She knew this was an automatic reaction most foals had when they were upset and insecure. She hoped it meant that Shadow was all right.

Ashleigh crammed her hands into her pockets and looked from her mother to her father. "Do you think Shadow's okay?" She bit her bottom lip and took a deep breath. If anything was wrong with the filly, it would be all her fault. Why hadn't she stopped to make sure Shadow had made it through the gate?

"I guess it didn't affect her appetite any," Mrs. Griffen said with a sigh of relief. "Let's get these two up to the barn and take a look at Shadow."

Ashleigh followed along and stood quietly while her parents examined the filly.

Mr. Griffen ran his hands over Shadow's front legs, lingering over the long cannon bones and tendons. Mrs. Griffen inspected the rest of her.

Ashleigh felt tears burning at the backs of her eyes. She'd never forgive herself if anything happened to Shadow!

Finally, after several long minutes, Mr. Griffen

stood, running a hand through his dark hair as he sighed. "So far, I can't find anything wrong with her."

Ashleigh let out her breath in a big whoosh.

"But that doesn't mean something might not show up in those tendons after she's stood for a while," Mr. Griffen warned. "Shadow's legs took a pretty hard beating on that wooden fence."

Ashleigh felt her insides twist. "What if there's permanent damage?" She knew her parents were counting on this special filly to bring a good price at auction as a yearling and grow Edgardale's reputation for raising good stock. If Shadow couldn't race, she'd bring a lot less money as a broodmare prospect.

Mrs. Griffen put her arm around Ashleigh's shoulders and gave her a squeeze. "I think she'll be okay," she reassured her. "But I hope you've learned something from this, Ashleigh. You've got to be careful and pay close attention when you're working with horses . . . especially the babies."

Ashleigh hung her head. She knew she'd let her parents down. They trusted her to help with the running of their farm. It was a big responsibility and one that she took seriously. She promised herself she'd be more cautious next time.

The sound of hoofbeats sounded outside the barn. "That must be Mona," Mr. Griffen said as he handed Go Gen's lead rope to Jonas. "There isn't anything you can do here, Ashleigh. Your chores are finished for now. You might as well go for a ride." He stood and offered her an encouraging smile. "Accidents happen. Just be more careful in the future."

Ashleigh nodded as she went to get Stardust ready. Her father was right. A ride was just what she needed. It would help her clear her thoughts. She clipped her chestnut mare into the crossties and sent Rory to tell Mona that she'd be out in a minute.

As Ashleigh walked Stardust out of the barn, her best friend, Mona Gardner, was waiting atop her own mare, Frisky. "Wow, you look really bummed," Mona said. "What happened?"

Ashleigh nodded to her friend, then led her mare to the mounting block and swung onto Stardust's back. "I'll tell you when we get out onto the trail," Ashleigh offered. "I really blew it today." She pointed her horse toward the trails and clucked her into a trot.

They rode in silence until they reached the field with the creek. Ashleigh pulled her mare up, then let her drop her head to eat. As Stardust happily cropped the short, autumn grass, Ashleigh thought about those high-class trainers who warned never to let your horse eat while you were riding. She liked to give her mare a treat. It made Stardust look forward to their rides. Ashleigh dismounted and stood beside her mare, absently stroking her glossy neck.

"So, what's up, Ash?" Mona asked as she gave Frisky enough rein to eat. The light bay Thoroughbred mare with the four white socks dropped her nose in the grass and began to crop.

Ashleigh smiled at Mona. They had been friends and neighbors forever. Ashleigh knew she could trust Mona not to judge what she had done. Ashleigh thanked her lucky stars that she had Mona as her best friend. What would she ever do without her? She quickly related the day's events.

"Wow. It's a miracle Shadow didn't break her leg," Mona said. "But it wasn't your fault, Ash," she added. "Weird things happen when you work with young horses. That's what my parents always say."

Ashleigh turned her face to the blue bowl of a sky as a flock of migrating ducks flew over in their V pattern. "If Shadow ends up okay, I'm going to ask my parents if we can keep her and raise her ourselves," she said, her face still pointing toward the sky.

"You're kidding!" Mona's jaw dropped open. "Your parents won't let you keep her—Shadow will bring too much money at the auction. Your parents need that money to keep Edgardale running and buy breedings to better stallions."

Ashleigh turned to Mona. A frown settled between her brows. "But we could make more money if we raced her ourselves!" she insisted. "Look at how much

Aladdin made by winning the Kentucky Derby. Shadow could even be the first filly to win the Triple Crown! That would give us enough money to do anything we want. My parents have got to see that."

Mona shrugged. "I don't know, Ash. Racing is so risky. There's never a guarantee."

"I know," Ashleigh said. "But I've got to try to talk my parents into this. Shadow is special. She'll win lots of big races. I just know it!"

"Speaking of races . . . ," Mona said. "Last one to the oak tree has to clean the other one's dirty tack!"

Ashleigh's head snapped up. "Let's go!" She accepted the challenge as she gathered her reins, put her foot into the stirrup of the English saddle, and swung onto Stardust's back. She pointed the little chestnut mare down the dirt path and let out a battle cry, urging Stardust to her top speed.

The girls raced down the path, dirt flying from their horses' heels as the wind whipped tears from their eyes. The two mares ran neck and neck while Ashleigh and Mona crouched low over their withers, smiling at each other as the landscape passed in a blur. They both understood the unwritten rule: They would reach the oak tree at the same time. They were both winners, and they were best friends for life!

"Tied again!" Ashleigh yelled as she stood in the irons like she had seen jockeys do at the racetrack.

Someday she was going to be riding real races. Until then, these practice runs with Mona would help her perfect her riding skills.

They pulled the excited horses down to a walk and turned them for home, listening to the steady cadence of their breathing as they walked the mares cool.

"The Keeneland yearling sale is only a couple of weeks away," Ashleigh reminded Mona. "Have you asked your parents if you can go with us?"

Mona nodded. "They said yes. I can hardly wait! Maybe this year one of Edgardale's yearlings will be a record breaker."

Ashleigh closed her eyes, swaying to the rhythm of Stardust's walk. She imagined the auction ring and all the wealthy buyers who attended the sale. Someday soon one of Edgardale's yearlings would be a top seller. Then maybe they'd have the money to race some of their own stock.

She opened her eyes and looked at Mona. "Gosh, I almost forgot. Today is the day we get to draw lots to see who gets to prepare each yearling for the sale. I hope I get Althea's yearling. That filly will look pretty in the blue ribbon I've been saving for her tail."

When they reached the edge of Mona's property, Ashleigh said good-bye to Mona, then rode on to Edgardale's big brown barn. She dismounted outside, then led Stardust into the barn. Ashleigh removed the mare's tack and brushed the dried sweat from her body.

"Come on, Ash!" Rory popped his red-gold head around the corner. "Mom and Dad are ready to draw the lots. And you got a package from Rhoda today. Come open it so I can see what's inside."

Ashleigh hurried to finish cleaning her mare and put her away. She wondered what Rhoda had sent. Rhoda was one of the Griffens' jockey friends. Rory ran ahead and retrieved the package from the office.

"Here, Ashleigh, open it now," Rory said.

Ashleigh tore open the box as she made her way to the office. She stopped in her tracks when she saw what was inside—jockey silks! Ashleigh pulled the faded red shirt from the box and smiled. This would be the perfect costume for the Halloween party. She joined the rest of the family in the barn's office, showing them the special present Rhoda had sent, then they got down to business. Everyone was ready to get started on this fun event. Even Caroline looked excited.

"Okay, everyone, gather around," Mr. Griffen said. "We've got the lots all written out." He held out several pieces of neatly cut typing paper.

Mrs. Griffen smiled. "Rory, you're going to team up with Ashleigh this year."

"Aw, I'm big enough to do this myself." Rory sulked.

"Maybe next year, champ." Mr. Griffen ruffled his son's hair. "We need you to help Ashleigh this time."

Rory looked up at his sister. "We'll have the best yearlings ever!" he promised Ashleigh.

Mr. Griffen fanned out the pieces of paper. Everyone picked their first round.

"I got Marvey Mary's colt," Caroline said.

Ashleigh showed their piece of paper to Rory. "We've got Slewette's filly."

Everyone smiled and prepared to make another draw. Ashleigh grinned as she grabbed her next choice. It didn't matter who she picked. She loved them all and would do her best to make them the finest-looking yearlings at the sale.

Ashleigh turned over her paper to see the next name, and suddenly the letters swam before her eyes. Her heart felt like someone had clamped a vise on it, and her next breath refused to come. There had to be a mistake. This couldn't be possible!

Her eyes darted quickly to her mother and father. In the space of a second she saw sympathy dawn in their eyes and knew there had been no mistake. She crumpled the piece of paper and threw it onto the straw-littered floor, then ran blindly out of the barn.

2

Rory bent to pick up the crumpled piece of paper. "It says Shadow," he exclaimed, proud of his ability to read. He glanced up in confusion. "Shadow's not a yearling."

Caroline looked at her parents for an explanation.

"We'll talk about this later, Caro," Mrs. Griffen said as she stared worriedly out the barn door. "Right now, we better go see about Ashleigh. I don't think she's taking this very well. She really loves that filly." She held out her hand to her husband, and together they went to find their youngest daughter.

Ashleigh heard the footsteps as her parents approached the feed shed where she was hiding. She squeezed down between the bags of grain, trying to make herself smaller. She dragged the sleeve of her shirt across her eyes, but it was no use. There were plenty more tears to wet her cheeks.

"Ashleigh?" Mr. Griffen's deep voice sounded gently from outside the shed. "We know you're in there. Why don't you come out so we can talk about this?"

Ashleigh sat where she was, aching so bad, she didn't dare move a muscle for fear she would fall apart. There just had to be a mistake! Shadow was only a weanling. She had at least another whole year at Edgardale. It had to be a cruel joke.

"Ashleigh?" Mrs. Griffen called. "Come on, honey. I know you're not very happy about this, but we need to talk about it. You can't just hide in the feed shed." She looked at her husband and squeezed his hand. "Your father and I want to discuss our decision with you. Please come out."

Ashleigh sniffed back a slew of tears and huffed. "You didn't discuss it with me before. What difference does it make now?" She gasped at her audacity. She was *never* allowed to talk back to her parents. She cringed as she waited for their reply. That outburst had probably cost her a week's worth of riding privileges.

"Ashleigh." Her father's voice sounded again, but he didn't seem angry, just exasperated.

Mrs. Griffen opened the feed shed door. "Ashleigh, you're a part of this family, and you help with the running of this breeding farm," she said. "We want you to understand the decisions we make."

Ashleigh paused. She wanted to understand them,

too. But what could possibly explain her parents selling Shadow at this early age? The Keeneland yearling sale was for *yearlings*. Shadow was only six months old.

Ashleigh unfolded her legs, wincing as the blood flowed back into them, making them tingle up and down. She brushed the hay stems from her pants and squinted as she stepped into the sunlight.

Mrs. Griffen reached out to wipe the trail of tears from Ashleigh's cheeks. Mr. Griffen put an arm around her shoulders and steered her toward the pen Shadow and Go Gen were in. They stood for a few minutes looking at the horses before Mr. Griffen took a deep breath and began.

"Ashleigh, we're a breeding farm operation," Mr. Griffen said. "That means we own a certain number of broodmares that we breed each year. We raise the foals and sell them off as yearlings. That's how we make our money. That's what puts food on the table and continues our operation here." He smiled gently at her. "It's the same routine every year. You know we can't keep them all."

Ashleigh stared at the beautiful black filly as she frisked next to her dam. "I don't want to keep them all—just one. And besides, Shadow is just about to be weaned. She's not supposed to be sold at auction for another year."

Mrs. Griffen nodded. "Yes, we are getting a little out

of sequence with Shadow, but we've had a call from a serious buyer. One of the big racing farms from southern Kentucky will be sending a man out for the auction. He wants to take a look at Shadow while he's here. We want to ready her along with the yearlings that are going to be sold."

Ashleigh felt like someone had punched her in the stomach. She knew the man would like Shadow. He'd have to be blind not to see her clean lines, great conformation, and spirit. She was as good as sold.

Shadow noticed Ashleigh standing by the fence. The filly tossed her head and nickered a greeting, then trotted up to the fence, turning to make sure her dam was following.

Ashleigh stepped forward and stroked Shadow's velvety soft nose, staring into her dark eyes. She felt another jolt of pain when she thought about the filly going to live with somebody else. She couldn't let that happen! She wouldn't give up Shadow without a fight!

She turned to face her parents. "Mom, Dad, if it's money you're worried about, Shadow will make lots of it. She's going to grow up to be a great racer, and she'll win all the big races." She saw the skeptical look in her parents' eyes. "Look how well Aladdin has done," Ashleigh defended. "He won the Kentucky Derby! Shadow is his full sister. She could do it, too!"

"Now, Ashleigh," Mrs. Griffen said. "You know there's no guarantee that Shadow will be the same horse that Aladdin is. Full brothers and sisters can be totally different horses." She turned to her husband. "We think Shadow is going to be a great racehorse, too. But anything can happen between now and the time she races."

Mr. Griffen squeezed Ashleigh's shoulders and gave her a sympathetic look. "You saw what happened this morning with Shadow. Racing is a big gamble. A horse's career can end as quickly as it starts. If we get a good offer on Shadow now, we've got to take it."

"Ashleigh," Mrs. Griffen said as she brushed a dark curl from Ashleigh's face. "I know Shadow has been very special to you, but you know we can't keep her. We'll make sure she goes to the right home. We want what is best for our stock."

Ashleigh wanted to scream that *keeping* Shadow would be what was best, but she knew it was no use. Her parents had made up their minds. She could only hope that something would happen to change that.

"We've got a little time before supper is ready," Mr. Griffen said. "Why don't you go visit Mona for a little bit? Maybe that will make you feel better."

Ashleigh nodded. Mona would understand how she felt. Maybe her friend could even help her figure out a way to convince her parents they were wrong.

She gave Shadow a final pat and cut across the Edgardale property to Mona's house.

Mona was out in the barn finishing her chores when Ashleigh arrived.

"What are you doing here?" she said as she looked up in surprise. "Did I forget about something? Were we supposed to do homework together tonight?"

Ashleigh grabbed the hay net that Mona was filling and held it open for her. "No, I just need a friend right now. You were right about my parents. They won't let me keep Shadow."

"I'm sorry, Ash. I know how special Shadow is to you. Let me finish with this hay net and we can go up to the house," Mona said as she reached for several large flakes of grass hay. She hung the net, then led the way out of the barn.

They entered the kitchen. Ashleigh's stomach growled at the hearty smell of roast beef.

Mona pulled two glasses from the cupboard. "I know it's before dinnertime, but my mom made some great chocolate chip cookies today. I don't think she'll mind if we have a couple." She pulled the milk from the fridge. "Besides, it's sort of an emergency. You need some big-time cheering up."

Ashleigh smiled. Just knowing that Mona cared made her feel better. They gathered their milk and cookies and headed upstairs to Mona's bedroom.

"So, what happened?" Mona took a big bite out of her cookie. "I guess your parents said no to keeping Shadow?"

Ashleigh's cookie felt like it went down sideways, lodging in her throat in a big lump. She washed it down with a gulp of cold milk. "It's so unfair!" Ashleigh said. "I mean, I know that we're a breeding farm, and we have to sell our yearlings to keep in business, but you'd think we could keep just one of them!"

Mona nodded in sympathy. "I don't know how you do it, Ash. They're not even my horses, and I get attached to them, too. It's sad to watch them grow and then see them go to somebody else."

Ashleigh left the remaining cookie on the plate. Her appetite was gone. "My parents are going to keep selling Edgardale babies. That much will never change," she said. "So maybe I should just stop caring about them. Maybe if I didn't get so involved with the horses, it wouldn't hurt so much when they leave." She looked up at Mona and saw the shocked look on her friend's face.

"You're not serious," Mona said. "You couldn't do that, Ash. Think of all the fun you would miss! Think of all the good times you've had over the years with all your foals. Besides," Mona reasoned. "If you didn't do all that horse stuff, you'd be just like Caroline. You wouldn't be *you*."

Ashleigh thought about that for a moment. She looked at Mona and grinned. "If I ever show up with my hair in curls and some yucky color of polish on my fingernails, promise me you'll lock me in the tack shed until I come to my senses!"

"It's a deal!" Mona said as they shook hands. They laughed, then Mona got serious. "I know it's hard, Ash, but don't waste the time you have left with Shadow. Love her as much as you can before she goes. Otherwise you might regret it when she's gone."

Ashleigh picked up the last cookie and stuffed it into her mouth. Mona was right. Shadow wasn't gone yet. They still had some good times to spend together. Something could still happen to change her parents' minds. She stood to leave. "Your family is coming over to help with the weaning tomorrow?" Ashleigh asked.

Mona nodded. "We'll be over as soon as we have breakfast."

Ashleigh left the house, waving good-bye as she trotted down the driveway. Her parents were right. She felt a little better now that she had talked to Mona. She was really lucky to have such a good friend.

Ashleigh woke on Sunday morning just as the sun was breaking over the horizon. She stretched, then snuggled back under the covers, relishing the warmth of the blankets on her body while the chilled autumn air nipped at her face. Her parents turned the heat down at night. The house didn't usually warm up until she came back from doing morning chores.

The whinny of a foal in the distance reminded Ashleigh that today was the day they would wean all the foals. She closed her eyes for a moment, but visions of Shadow struggling to get over the fence passed before her eyes. Ashleigh sighed. She hoped the separation would go easy for the filly.

The sound of footsteps echoed from downstairs, and a moment later the heater kicked on. Ashleigh smiled as she snuggled even deeper into the covers. She'd wait just a few more minutes, until a little more heat seeped into the house, then she'd get up and grab a quick breakfast and go help Jonas with the morning chores.

Jonas was just setting out the feed buckets when Ashleigh arrived at the barn. "Today's the big day," he said as he handed a container of vitamins to Ashleigh.

Ashleigh measured a scoop and poured it over the first bucket of grain. "I hope we don't have any trouble with Shadow today."

"I think she'll do all right," Jonas reassured her. "Her legs look good this morning. Yesterday's fiasco didn't seem to harm her any."

Ashleigh took the first bucket of grain to Stardust. The chestnut mare nickered a greeting and stepped back to let Ashleigh into the stall.

"Sorry, it's not as much as the broodmares get," she apologized to Stardust as she dumped the grain into the feeder on the wall. "But if I give you too much, you'll have so much energy, you might want to throw me off."

Stardust blew through her lips, then dug into the feeder of oats. Ashleigh laughed. "Yeah, I'd be walking home from that old oak tree if you got as much grain as the broodmares."

She patted her mare, then returned to help Jonas with the rest of the horses. Moe, Rory's fat little molasses-colored pony, called to Ashleigh as she dumped grain into Althea's stall. "Sorry, Moe," Ashleigh said. "All you get is a handful." She laughed as the pony lipped every piece of grain out of her palm.

It wasn't long until the rest of the Griffen family made their way out to the barn. Mona and her mom and dad arrived just before nine.

"Let's get started," Mr. Griffen said as he handed the broodmare halters to the adults and the foal halters to the kids. "Ashleigh, I want you and Mona to work with one of us adults. You girls go into the stalls and halter the babies, then turn the lead rope over to one of us. You can walk alongside the mares as we go to the weaning pen, but stay out of the way. You know how crazy things can get."

Mrs. Griffen motioned for Mona to follow her. "Caroline and Rory will work the gates. You know the routine," she said. "When we get to the weaning pen, we'll put the foal in and take off the halter."

They took the first two mares and foals out together so that none of the weanlings would be in the pen by themselves. Jolita and her leggy filly were the next to go, followed by My Georgina and her colt.

It wasn't long until the sound of distressed mares and foals filled the air. Mares called to their foals and ran up and down the fence line while the newly weaned fillies and colts streaked across the weaning pen, kicking up their heels and shaking their heads in protest.

Ashleigh knew the noise would continue throughout the day and night. By the time she got home from school the next day, most of the horses would be settling into the new arrangement, and the weanlings would start getting used to having each other as steady companions.

Shadow and Go Gen were the last pair to be separated. Ashleigh walked into the stall and slipped the halter over Shadow's elegant head. "Don't worry," Ashleigh said. "It's going to be all right. In another day or two you'll get used to having your mom gone.

You'll have fun playing with all the other weanlings."

Caroline opened the stall door. Mr. Griffen walked Go Gen through the opening. Ashleigh paused before handing off the lead rope to her mother. "Shadow's behaving very well. Can I walk her out to the pen?"

Mrs. Griffen hesitated, looking at her husband. "What do you think, Derek? They seem to be going calmly. I think Ashleigh can handle this."

At her husband's nod, she smiled at Ashleigh. "Just be careful," she warned. "Things can turn to trouble in a hurry."

Ashleigh grinned as she led Shadow out the door. She spoke calmly to the filly as they walked toward the pen, with Mona following beside them. When they reached their destination, Caroline opened the gate and Ashleigh and Mona walked Shadow inside.

The other foals started forward. Mona stepped toward them, stretching her arms out to her sides. "I'll herd them toward the back of the pen until you set Shadow free," she offered.

"Get the halter off that filly and get out of there before she starts raising a fuss," Mr. Griffen said as he led Go Gen away.

Shadow stood like a statue, her head held high as she watched her dam go. The only hint of her concern was the twitching of her muscles as Go Gen got farther away.

"Better get the halter off her while she's standing so well," Mona said as she looked back over her shoulder to see what Ashleigh was doing.

Ashleigh stepped forward to remove the halter just as Shadow sprang into action, lunging toward the closed gate.

"Whoa!" Caroline yelled as she stepped back quickly in case Shadow decided to repeat yesterday's performance.

Ashleigh's heart jumped in her chest as Shadow banged against the wooden gate. She couldn't let the filly attempt the fence. They might not be so lucky this time. She wrapped the lead rope around her hand to get a better hold. She knew this was dangerous— she could be dragged. But her only thought at the moment was to stop Shadow from hurting herself.

"Whoa, Shadow!" Ashleigh cried as the filly charged the fence, jerking the lead rope tight around Ashleigh's balled fist.

"Get that halter off now, Ash!" Caroline called from outside the pen.

"I'm trying," Ashleigh gritted out as she took another wrap on the lead rope, jerking Shadow's head around. Her arms ached under the strain of the filly's pull. "Come on, Shadow," she pleaded.

Shadow hesitated at the sound of Ashleigh's voice, her ears flicking forward.

"Hurry, Ash," Mona said. "The other foals want to see what's happening. I won't be able to keep them back much longer."

"Good girl." Ashleigh breathed a sigh of relief as she stepped forward to remove the halter.

The call of a mare sounded in the distance. Ashleigh cried out in pain as Shadow exploded, rearing high into the air and jerking Ashleigh forward. Shadow shied, diving to the side before bolting away.

With the rope caught around her hand, Ashleigh had no choice but to stumble along behind the filly, her heart beating wildly as she struggled to free herself. Shadow wasn't very big, but she was strong enough to pull Ashleigh along.

Ashleigh felt the burn of the cotton lead across her palm as she tried desperately to get loose, but she knew it was no use—she was hopelessly caught in the line.

3

Ashleigh winced as the lead rope tightened on her hand, refusing to slide free.

"Ashleigh, look out!" Mona cried as she dashed forward, waving her arms in Shadow's face.

The filly slid to a halt just inches from Mona. With the line now slack, Ashleigh quickly freed her hand from the rope at the same time Mona reached out to unbuckle Shadow's halter. The filly dashed away, running to join the other weanlings.

Caroline sprinted into the pen. "Are you okay?"

Ashleigh raised an unsteady hand to brush her tangled hair out of her face. "I—I think so," she stammered, hardly recognizing her own voice, it was quivering so much.

"Are you hurt?" Caroline said with a worried frown.

Ashleigh looked at her palms. They were a little red

from the friction of the rope, but otherwise she was okay. "I'm all right," she said glancing nervously toward the stables. "Mom and Dad were already up at the barn when Shadow took off. I don't think they saw. Let's not tell them what happened, okay?" She looked from Mona to Caroline.

Everyone nodded in agreement.

Ashleigh smiled at Mona. "You stepped in front of Shadow," she said in amazement. "You could have been hurt, but you did it to save me."

Mona kicked at the dirt. "You would have done the same for me, Ash."

"Don't be so modest." Caroline chuckled. "You did a very brave thing. Too bad we can't tell anyone about it."

Mona shrugged. "She's my best friend."

Ashleigh smiled and slapped her friend a high five, flinching at the pain that raced up her hand. "I'm glad we're best friends," she said.

"Yeah, best friends for life!" Mona agreed.

Ashleigh took the empty halter and lead rope from Mona and walked toward the gate. "We better hurry back to the barn before somebody comes to see what's taking so long."

Together they walked back to the stable, talking about anything except the serious accident Ashleigh had narrowly avoided.

Mr. Griffen stepped from the stable doorway as they approached. "Looks like another year of successful weaning," he said. "You kids go on up to the house. We'll be up as soon as we do one more check on the mares and foals."

"Caroline," Mrs. Griffen called over her shoulder as she headed for the broodmare pen. "Could you please start lunch? This crew looks pretty hungry."

Ashleigh turned to follow her sister toward their white, two-story farmhouse. In the distance she could hear the frantic whinny of the newly weaned foals. One frightened call sounded more desperate than all the rest. She knew that one was Shadow.

The following week passed in a blur as everyone at Edgardale worked hard to prepare their yearlings for the sale. Manes had to be pulled, whiskers clipped, and feet trimmed. The Keeneland sale ran for eleven whole days, but Edgardale's yearlings were all selling in the last four days of the auction. They would be shipped to Keeneland the following week.

Ashleigh and Rory made a pact that their yearlings were going to be the best ones of the bunch. Every day they brushed coats until they glistened. Any spare time that Ashleigh had, she split between Stardust and

Shadow. The filly had finally gotten over missing her mother and was starting to respond well to her lessons.

Earlier in the week Melvin McPhearson from Eagle Brook Farm had called to make an appointment to see Shadow. He would be arriving later in the day. Ashleigh picked a small blue halter off the wall and went to get the filly.

She stood outside the gate of the weanling pen, watching as Shadow frisked with the other colts and fillies. Her throat tightened as she thought about all her plans for raising and racing Shadow. Those dreams were all being smashed to pieces.

"Don't be sad, Ashleigh," Rory said as he came to stand beside her and took her hand, smudging part of his melted chocolate bar onto her fingers as he tried to give her comfort.

Ashleigh smiled at her little brother as she extracted her hand and wiped it on her jeans. "I can't help it, Rory. Shadow is my favorite. It's not fair! We always get to keep the foals until they're yearlings. Why do we have to sell Shadow now?"

Rory stared into the pasture, his mouth turned down in a frown. Suddenly he brightened. "Hey, maybe the man won't like Shadow. Then she can stay with us for another year!"

Ashleigh ruffled Rory's red-gold hair, then raised

her fingers to her lips and whistled. She smiled as Shadow stopped midplay and sounded a greeting before dashing toward them.

"Look at her go!" Ashleigh said with pride. "See how she flows across the ground, Rory? Even though she's smaller than the rest of them, she's still at the front of the pack." She shook her head and sighed. "Mr. McPhearson really knows his horses. Eagle Brook has produced several Kentucky Derby winners. He'll know Shadow is special when he sees her."

Shadow slid to a halt before she reached the gate, then stepped forward and nickered. Ashleigh smirked. At least the filly had learned her lesson about jumping fences. Ashleigh opened the gate and put the halter on the filly. Shadow lipped the front of her shirt and nuzzled her cheek. Ashleigh felt the tears building behind her eyes. Mr. McPhearson was a smart man. Shadow was as good as gone.

She led the filly to the barn and hooked her into the crossties.

Jonas stepped from the tack room. He removed his hat, scratching his graying head as he studied Ashleigh. "Don't look so down," he said. "Edgardale should be honored to have one of their horses come to the notice of Melvin McPhearson. If he decides to buy this filly, he'll do right by her."

Ashleigh grabbed up a hoof pick and began her

grooming routine. "I've heard good things about Mr. McPhearson," she said, hoping to lure Jonas into a conversation. The old stable hand didn't talk a whole lot, but when he did, he usually had something interesting to say.

Jonas leaned against the wall and stuck a blade of hay between his teeth. "I've been to his place. Seen the man in action," Jonas volunteered.

Ashleigh dropped Shadow's hoof and stood. "You have?"

Jonas nodded. "I was working down that way. One of his grooms got hurt. He needed temporary help, so I filled in for a couple of weeks." Jonas looked at Ashleigh over the top of Shadow's back. "I know you and this filly have got something special, and you're hurting really bad just thinking about her going. But this is a breeding farm, Ashleigh. It's the nature of the business."

Ashleigh stood silent as she watched Jonas turn to leave. "But how do you do it?" she called after him. "How do you *not* hurt?"

Jonas stopped in the middle of the aisle and turned to Ashleigh. "That's something you've got to figure out for yourself, missy. I can't help you out with that one."

Ashleigh watched Jonas shuffle down the way and disappear around the corner. She picked up a rubber currycomb and rubbed it in circles across Shadow's coat. Jonas was right. She had to learn to get control of her emotions. Edgardale sold ten yearlings per year. They had bought a new broodmare at the start of this past breeding season and were planning to buy a couple more. If she fell in love with all of them, she'd be a total wreck by the time she was a teenager. Maybe Caroline had it right, Ashleigh thought. Caro never got too attached to any of the horses.

Ashleigh worked furiously on Shadow, running the soft body brush over her coat, then flicking the dust rag over her from head to tail until her coat shown a blue-black color. She stood back to admire her handiwork just as her mother poked her head through the barn door.

"He's here, Ashleigh," Mrs. Griffen said. "Put the leather halter on Shadow. Your father will be in to get her in a minute."

Ashleigh sucked in her breath as her stomach did a quick flop. This was it! Shadow's fate could be determined in the next half hour. She felt the panic welling up inside her as she reached for the leather halter. Her hands shook as she undid the blue nylon one and fastened it around Shadow's neck so she could slip the fancy headstall into place.

A million thoughts ran through her head. Maybe if she were to set Shadow free, the filly would run to one of the far fields and they wouldn't be able to find her until after Mr. McPhearson had left. She started to unbuckle the holding halter from around Shadow's neck, but the sound of footfalls outside the barn door jolted Ashleigh to her senses. This was a big opportunity for Edgardale. Her parents would never forgive her if she messed this one up.

Ashleigh put aside her selfish feelings and quickly slipped the leather halter over Shadow's elegant head, handing the lead line to her father as he walked through the door.

"She looks great, Ashleigh," Mr. Griffen said with a smile as he patted Ashleigh on the back. He gave her shoulder a squeeze. "I know how hard this is for you, honey, but if this man buys Shadow, it could be a real boost for Edgardale. He could help put us on the map with the other big breeding farms."

Ashleigh tucked her hair behind her ears and attempted a smile even though her heart was breaking. "I know, Dad." She pushed her hands deep into the pockets of her jeans and followed her father and Shadow out the door.

Ashleigh blinked as she stepped into the bright autumn sunlight. When the dots stopped swimming before her eyes, she came to focus on the man standing in the driveway. He reminded her of a comic book character. He was at least six inches taller than her father, and her father was an average-size man. The stranger was as skinny as a jockey and had hawklike features with high cheekbones and a long, sharp nose. Ashleigh guessed him to be in his midforties, but he still had bright blond hair.

She was surprised when he turned to look at her and smiled. Ashleigh had expected a harsh grimace, but his smile lit up his entire face, and his warm blue eyes made her feel like smiling back at him. She wanted to hate the man for coming to look at her horse, but she found herself smiling back at Melvin McPhearson.

"Mr. McPhearson, this is our daughter Ashleigh," Mr. Griffen said. "Shadow is her special filly. Ashleigh's done most of the work with her, including foaling her during a snowstorm."

"I'm impressed," Melvin McPhearson said as he stepped forward to shake Ashleigh's hand. "Your mother and father are starting to build a good reputation in the breeding field. If you keep working with them, there'll be lots of big farms looking to hire you when you're out of school."

Mrs. Griffen stepped forward and took Shadow from her husband, squaring the filly up on all four legs while he handed the filly's pedigree to Mr. McPhearson. "Ashleigh wants to be a jockey," she said, looking proudly at her youngest daughter.

"Is that right?" Melvin McPhearson glanced at Ashleigh over the top of the pedigree. He nodded. "You look like you're going to be about the right size. Eagle Brook is always looking for fresh talent. I'd be happy to help you get started if you ever find yourself down our way."

Ashleigh smiled at the man. He was making it very hard for her to dislike him. She turned and sat in the shade of the trees while her parents went about the business of showing Shadow.

After a half hour of running his hands over every inch of the black filly and watching her move, Mr. McPhearson scratched his chin. "I'll be in touch," he said. With a nod to her folks, he hopped into his new pickup truck and drove off down the long, winding gravel drive.

"Well, what do you think?" Elaine Griffen asked her husband. "He left awfully fast."

Mr. Griffen shrugged. "I don't know. He seemed to like her. I guess we'll just have to wait and see."

Ashleigh stepped from the shade of the oak trees and took Shadow's lead rope, walking the filly back to her pen. She knew Mr. McPhearson would be back. Shadow was as good as sold.

●   ●   ●

The following week was torture for Ashleigh. Christmas and Thanksgiving were just around the corner, and preparations had already been started for a big Halloween party at Jamie's house. Ashleigh couldn't wait to wear her jockey costume.

The yearlings had been moved to Keeneland several days earlier so prospective buyers could look at them before the sale, and Ashleigh missed them terribly. The auction had already started, and prices were up. That was good news for Edgardale, but Ashleigh took no joy in it. She jumped every time the phone rang, worrying that it would be Mr. McPhearson calling to make an appointment to come get Shadow. She knew the call was coming. It was just a matter of when.

After several days had passed and nothing was heard from Eagle Brook's manager, Ashleigh began to hope that he wouldn't call. But the phone rang during supper midweek, and Ashleigh knew by the way her mother's eyes cut quickly in her direction that the call was from Melvin McPhearson and that Shadow was no longer theirs.

"That was Mr. McPhearson," Elaine Griffen said as she hung up the phone. "He's agreed to our asking price. He'll be here tomorrow morning to load Shadow and settle up."

Ashleigh felt all eyes turn in her direction. The chicken potpie she had just eaten lay like a brick in her stomach. She took a deep breath, holding it to stop the tears from coming. She had known this moment would arrive. She had tried to prepare herself, but it was no use. She could feel her heart being torn in two. It wasn't fair! Shadow was her favorite.

Ashleigh folded her napkin, looking at each of the sympathetic faces staring in her direction. Rory's bottom lip began to quiver, and she knew that if she kept looking at him, she would burst into tears.

Ashleigh stood quickly. Her chair made a loud crash as it toppled over backward. She ran from the table without being excused. She knew it was rude, but at the moment she didn't care if she got grounded for life.

Ashleigh took the stairs two at a time, barging into her bedroom and slamming the door behind her before dropping onto her bed and crying into her pillow.

She didn't know how long she lay there. One by one, her family came to check on her, but she motioned them away, softly crying into her pillow until the tears refused to come anymore.

Ashleigh lay in the dark, listening to the sounds of the night chores being done. The last time Caroline had checked in on her, she had told Ashleigh that she would do her share of the chores.

Ashleigh listened intently to the sounds of the old

house as she lay in the dark. There were a few creaks, but she was sure no one else was in the house. While she had been lying there, a plan had formed in her mind. She couldn't give up Shadow without a fight!

She ran the back of her hand over her eyes and got off the bed, making her way carefully down the darkened staircase. She reached the living room and picked up the phone, dialing Mona's house. After several rings her friend answered the phone.

"Who is this?" Mona said, not recognizing Ashleigh's hoarse voice.

"It's me, Mona," Ashleigh said.

"What happened? You sound awful!" Mona's voice was full of concern.

"Mr. McPhearson is buying Shadow," Ashleigh explained. "I've only got a minute until my family comes back into the house. You've got to listen closely." She hesitated, knowing that what she was about to do was crazy and could get her into lots of trouble. She hurried on before she lost her courage. "I need you to meet me by the big oak tree in the back pasture tomorrow before school. Be there at dawn. I've got a plan. . . ."

4

Ashleigh reached for the off button as soon as the alarm sounded at five o'clock in the morning. It was still dark outside—just like she had intended it to be. The alarm had barely made a squeak, but Caroline rolled over in her bed.

"Is it time to get up already?" She groaned.

"No, Caro. The alarm was set wrong," Ashleigh said. "It's Saturday. We don't have to get up for a couple more hours. Go back to sleep."

Ashleigh lay there until she heard the even rhythm of her sister's breathing, then she quietly slipped out of bed and pulled on her jeans and a sweatshirt. The fall mornings were getting quite chilly. She grabbed her boots and tiptoed down the staircase, heading for the back door since it was the farthest from her parents' bedroom.

Ashleigh stepped out into the night, breathing

deeply the crisp Kentucky air. She could smell the lingering smoke of autumn leaves that their neighbors had burned yesterday. She smiled. It wouldn't be long now until their Halloween party. She couldn't wait to wear her jockey costume. From now until the end of the year, there would be a series of fun parties.

Ashleigh sat down on the steps and quickly pulled on her boots, then ran across the dew-covered grass toward the barn. The moon was still up, and it was almost full. Ashleigh grinned. The extra light would help her with her plan.

She slowed as she approached the barn. The next problem was going to be slipping into the stable to retrieve a halter without waking Jonas. She knew her mare, Stardust, and all the broodmares would nicker a greeting when they saw her. Why hadn't she thought to put the halter out last night?

Ashleigh knew she couldn't afford to get caught. Her parents wouldn't understand that she was trying to do what was best for Edgardale. If they found out that she was responsible for this stunt, she wouldn't get to attend any of the holiday parties. She had to make this look like an accident.

Ashleigh slowly opened the barn door. She stepped into the cool stable, inhaling all the warm horse smells. Her breath caught in her throat when Stardust poked her head over the stall door and whinnied. Ashleigh quickly backed out of the barn and closed the door. She watched to see if the light would come on in Jonas's overhead apartment. After several minutes it still remained dark. She breathed a sigh of relief.

Ashleigh rubbed her hands together as she stared around the moonlit barnyard. How was she going to get that halter and lead rope without waking Jonas? Her eyes passed over the dark silhouette of their horse trailer, and she brightened. Her parents always kept extra halters in the horse trailer in case they needed them on the road.

She ran to the trailer and opened the side door, cringing when it squeaked on its hinges. She fumbled around in the dark interior, smiling when her hand landed on a halter and lead rope. She quickly closed the door and made her way to the weanling pen.

The weanlings nickered nervously and snorted when she entered their pen. "Easy, guys," Ashleigh crooned as she walked forward cautiously. She didn't want to spook them and cause a stampede. In the glowing light of the moon she could make out Shadow's three white socks and blazed face. "Here, girl," she said as she held out her hand and slowly approached the filly.

Shadow sniffed the air, then, recognizing Ashleigh's scent, she bobbed her head and moved forward.

"Good girl," Ashleigh said as she slipped the halter

over Shadow's nose. "Let's get out of here as quietly as we can."

Ashleigh slowly opened the gate, shooing back the other weanlings that tried to follow. She pulled Shadow through the opening and breathed a sigh of relief when the gate clicked softly closed behind them. She couldn't believe she had actually made it this far.

Ashleigh paused for a moment, stroking Shadow's silky black coat. Misgivings began to creep into her thoughts. The reason she hadn't told Mona about her plan was because she knew her friend would have tried to talk her out of it.

Ashleigh looked toward the field where Mona would be waiting for her. She hesitated again. Her stomach began to roll. If she got caught, she would be in more trouble than she had ever been in before. Mr. McPhearson had offered a lot of money for Shadow.

Shadow seemed to sense Ashleigh's unease. The filly poked her nose at her and ran her whiskers across her cheek.

"What are you trying to tell me, girl?" Ashleigh rubbed her hands on either side of the filly's jawbones and kissed her velvety muzzle. She could see the reflection of the moonlight in the filly's gentle eyes. "You don't want to leave here, do you, girl?"

Shadow blew through her lips and nibbled at Ashleigh's sweatshirt.

"Okay, you convinced me," Ashleigh said as she tugged on the lead rope and started off toward the field where Mona would be waiting under the old oak tree.

Several of the weanlings whinnied and trotted up and down the fence line when Ashleigh led Shadow away. Shadow stopped and looked back, nickering to her friends. For a moment Ashleigh thought there was going to be a problem, then Shadow moved forward at the tug on the lead rope, and Ashleigh's worries disappeared.

They skirted down the side of the driveway, trying to avoid crossing the gravel driveway until they were out of hearing range of the house and barn. It took them a little out of their way, but the extra time was worth eliminating the risk of making too much noise on the crunchy gravel. When they got to the field path, Ashleigh picked up the pace, hurrying to where Mona waited.

"Ashleigh?" Mona called out when she saw their silhouettes approach.

"Yeah, it's me," Ashleigh answered as she slowed to a walk.

"What are you doing with Shadow?" Mona said as she stepped from under the tree.

Ashleigh saw the worried look on her friend's face. She paused for a moment to catch her breath, then filled Mona in on her plan. "Mr. McPhearson is supposed to be here at nine o' clock to pick up Shadow. I want to take her into the very back fields and hide her someplace where nobody can find her. After a while Mr. McPhearson will get tired of waiting, and he'll go home. If he withdraws his offer, then we'll be able to keep Shadow."

Ashleigh peered through the faint light, trying to read her friend's face. Even in the semidarkness Ashleigh could see that Mona wasn't impressed.

"Are you out of your mind, Ash?" Mona's voice exploded into the quiet of the early dawn.

Ashleigh felt the sting of Mona's words. Her friend was supposed to be *helping* her, not handing out insults. "It will work," Ashleigh insisted.

Mona put a hand on Ashleigh's arm. "Ash, think about this really hard before you do it. Shadow is worth a lot of money—more than you've gotten for any of the yearlings you've run through the sales. Do you have any idea what your parents will do to you if you mess that up?" She shook her head in exasperation. "You'll be grounded for life!"

"No," Ashleigh assured her. "They won't know I did it. It'll look like an accident." Ashleigh saw the skeptical look in her friend's eyes and continued. "My parents know that Shadow likes to jump fences when she's scared. They'll just think she's jumped the fence and gone. Once Mr. McPhearson has left, I'll take Stardust out for a ride and say that I found Shadow."

Mona sat down on a tree stump. She put her head in her hands and sighed. "Ashleigh, I've known you all my life, and this is the craziest thing you've ever done." She stared off into the distance at the rising sun, then looked back at her friend. "Don't do this," she begged. "Think of all the fun things you'll miss out on if you get grounded. The holidays are coming up. You'll miss all the good stuff."

"But my parents won't know," Ashleigh insisted. "I won't get caught, and we'll get to keep Shadow. Don't you get it? It will all work out perfect."

Mona groaned. "It won't save Shadow, Ash. Don't you see? What's to stop Mr. McPhearson from coming back the next day or the next week? If he's willing to pay that much money for Shadow, he'll still want her when she turns up. You can't hide her forever. Please, Ash," Mona begged. "For your own sake. Don't do this."

Ashleigh felt the desperation building inside her. The burn of tears pricked behind her eyes. She took a deep breath, then turned on Mona. "You're supposed to be my best friend!" she accused. "Why are you being so mean?" Ashleigh felt the tears roll down her cheeks. She couldn't stop them. She tried to speak, but a sob came out instead.

Shadow caught Ashleigh's unease and began to

dance around at the end of the lead line. Ashleigh hiccuped several times as she tried to get herself and the filly under control. She turned back to Mona. "You know how much I love Shadow. I don't want to lose her! Why won't you help me?"

Mona rose from the tree stump and went to Ashleigh. "You're my best friend, Ash—"

Ashleigh cut off Mona's speech. "How can you say that when you won't help me?" She hated the ugly tone she heard in her own voice, but she couldn't stop it. She was hurting so bad right now, she just wanted to lash out at Mona.

"Think about it, Ash," Mona pleaded. "You know this won't work. What happens if your parents find Shadow tied up in the back field? They'll *know* it was you. And what if Shadow gets hurt back there? Think of everything you've got to lose." She paused, waiting to see if her words were sinking in. "You'll be grounded from the horses and all after-school activities if you get caught. The Halloween party is coming up. We had a lot of plans. . . ."

Ashleigh threw her arms around Shadow's neck, rubbing her tears into the filly's silky mane. "But we won't get caught," she said trying to convince herself but already beginning to see Mona's point and hating it. Giving up this plan meant giving up Shadow, and she wasn't ready to do that.

"But you *will* get caught, Ash," Mona said. "I don't know how this plan can work. And how would you feel if Shadow got seriously hurt and couldn't ever race?" She put her hand on Ashleigh's shoulder. "At least you know Mr. McPhearson will give her a good home. He's a great trainer. You'll be able to go see her race. If anybody can get Shadow to the big races, it's Melvin McPhearson."

Ashleigh sniffed. She knew her friend was right. But just knowing that she had to take Shadow back to the barn made her heart feel like it was being crushed.

"Maybe someday when you're a jockey, you'll be able to ride Shadow in a race," Mona offered.

Ashleigh felt the corners of her mouth turn up. That was a good thought. In another three years she would be old enough and strong enough to start learning how to gallop racehorses. Mr. McPhearson had offered to give her a chance. Maybe she could talk her parents into taking her to visit his farm some summer.

"Come on, Ash." Mona tugged on her arm. "Let's get this filly back to the barn before your parents know she's gone."

Ashleigh lifted her cheek from Shadow's mane and stared at the golden sunrise. The birds were beginning to sing, and the bark of dogs could be heard in the distance. She glanced at Mona, then looked down at the ground. "I'm really sorry I yelled at you. I didn't mean to. I just . . . "

"It's okay." Mona waved off the apology. "I know how much this hurts. I just wish there was some way I could make it better."

Ashleigh smiled at her friend. "You already have," she said. "Just being my friend—even when I'm a jerk—helps a lot." Ashleigh drew a deep breath. "I think you've just saved me from the biggest grounding I've ever had."

They laughed as they turned back toward Edgardale. Ashleigh winced. She had cried so much, it hurt her ribs to chuckle, but she had to find some sense of mirth in this whole thing. Otherwise she'd go back to crying again.

"Oh, no," Ashleigh said as Edgardale came into view. "It looks like my parents are up and helping Jonas feed. What are we going to do?"

"Maybe we can walk around the back way and sneak Shadow into her pen," Mona said.

They cut through the field and down the side of the barn. They were almost to the weanling pen when Mrs. Griffen rounded the corner with a wheelbarrow full of hay for the colts and fillies.

Elaine Griffen stopped in her tracks. A look of curiosity came over her face. It was quickly replaced by a wary stare. "What are you doing, Ashleigh?" She glanced at the direction they had come from. "What's going on?"

Ashleigh felt her stomach flop. Her mind spun as she tried to think of something to say. She was going to get into trouble after all.

Mona stepped forward. "Ashleigh wanted to take one last walk with Shadow before she left," she explained.

Mrs. Griffen looked from Mona to Ashleigh. "You must have gotten up awfully early. Why not wait until after Shadow had her breakfast?"

Ashleigh could hear the suspicion in her mother's words. She searched for something to say, but it felt like her voice was stuck.

"We decided to do it early so Shadow could be ready to go when Mr. McPhearson got here," Mona volunteered. She poked Ashleigh in the ribs when Mrs. Griffen turned her head.

Ashleigh jumped and gave Mona a warning frown as she rubbed her sore ribs. "Yeah, I just wanted to spend some quiet time with Shadow away from everyone," Ashleigh agreed. "I'll put her back in with the others now."

Ashleigh led Shadow back to her pen. The other colts and fillies ran to the fence to greet her. Shadow cocked her tail over her back and pranced through the herd, her head held high.

"She's so beautiful," Mona said.

Ashleigh turned from the pen and walked back toward the barn. She could feel her tears welling up again. "It's hard to believe she's going to be gone in a couple more hours." She looked over her shoulder to watch Shadow bully her way to the hay pile. At least the filly was learning how to take care of herself, she thought. She'd need to be able to do that once she was at her new home and Ashleigh wasn't there to look after her.

"Want to come over to my house?" Mona asked. "Maybe it would be better if you weren't here to see her go."

Ashleigh shook her head. "I've got to be here to say good-bye."

Mona nodded in understanding. They returned the halter and lead rope to the horse trailer, then helped Ashleigh's family finish the rest of the chores.

Mrs. Griffen entered the stall Ashleigh and Mona were mucking out. "Here, Ashleigh," she said as she handed Ashleigh a bunch of carrots. "Why don't you go spend the rest of your time with Shadow? Rory and Caroline can finish your stalls."

Caroline took the pitchfork from her hands and gave her a sympathetic smile. "Go on, Ash. We'll finish up."

Rory just stared at her with big, blue eyes that looked like they were about to spill over with fresh tears.

Ashleigh was afraid to say anything for fear she would start crying again. She just nodded, put the carrots in her pocket, and walked out of the stall.

Mona followed her out of the barn. "Look, Ash, I know you want to be alone with Shadow right now. I'll just say a quick good-bye to her, then I'll go home. If it will make you feel better, we can go for a ride after Shadow leaves."

Ashleigh smiled at her friend. "Maybe we can ride up by the pond. It's quiet there. We can talk about all the foals we're going to raise and race when we grow up."

Mona nodded. "Just come over to my house when you're ready."

Ashleigh waited for her friend to leave, then she entered Shadow's pen. "I've got something for you," she said as she held out the carrots. All the other weanlings recognized the treat and came forward, pushing each other to get closer to her.

Ashleigh smiled. She should have known better than to advertise. Everyone wanted a share of Shadow's carrots. She broke them into enough pieces so that each weanling could have some. "Guess this is your going-away party, girl," Ashleigh said as she raised her hand to brush away a tear.

Shadow nuzzled her hand, looking for more to eat.

It was more than Ashleigh could stand. She threw her arms around Shadow's neck and let her tears flow freely. A moment later she heard the rattle of a horse trailer as it made its way down Edgardale's long gravel driveway.

5

Ashleigh's head snapped up when she heard the slamming of the pickup door, signaling Mr. McPhearson was ready to do business. She stayed where she was, hugging Shadow even tighter as she waited for the adults to handle all the paperwork. She wanted to spend every last second with her filly.

Ashleigh's mind flashed back to the night Shadow had been born. It had been so cold, and she was so scared. She had helped the filly take her first steps and watched her drink her first meal. But now Shadow was going to live somewhere else, and Ashleigh couldn't be sure she'd ever see the filly again.

"I'm going to miss you so much," she cried.

Shadow's ears flicked back and forth at the sound of Ashleigh's sobs, but the filly stood still, seeming to sense that something big was happening.

"Except for Stardust, I'll never love another horse like I do you," Ashleigh promised.

The rest of the weanlings crept closer, picking at Ashleigh's clothing, trying to draw her attention, but she ignored them all. She didn't want to see any of their sweet faces or look into their inquisitive eyes. She wasn't going to get attached to any of them. It hurt too much when they had to leave. And Ashleigh knew that *all* of them would be leaving. This was a broodmare farm, not a racing farm.

Maybe Caroline had it right, Ashleigh thought. She never got too attached to any of the horses. Ashleigh had always thought that Caroline was crazy to be able to live on such a great horse farm and not like any of the horses. But at least her sister didn't have a broken heart every year when the yearlings were sold. Maybe she should start being more like her sister.

"Ashleigh," Mrs. Griffen's voice called from over the fence. "It's time. Could you please bring Shadow up to the barn? Mr. McPhearson is ready to load her up." She gave Ashleigh a sympathetic smile. "Would you like me to do it, dear? Would it be easier on you?"

Ashleigh straightened and brushed the sleeve of her sweatshirt across her eyes. She took a deep breath and shook her head. "No, Mom. I want to do it. She knows me the best. She'll load better in the trailer if I'm there with her."

Mrs. Griffen nodded in understanding as she opened the gate.

Ashleigh's feet felt like posts in cement as she forced herself to put one foot in front of the other. She couldn't cry anymore. She had exhausted all her tears.

Melvin McPhearson smiled as Ashleigh brought Shadow into the stable yard. Ashleigh tried to return the smile as she handed him the lead rope. "She'll make you a great champion filly," she said, desperately hoping that her voice wouldn't crack and give away just how much this was costing her.

Mr. McPhearson patted Ashleigh on the shoulder. "I'm sure she will. I believe in the faith you have in this filly. You've got a good eye, missy." He handed Ashleigh a business card with Eagle Brook's phone number on it. "You be sure to call me any time you want to check on this filly's progress," he said. "And you're welcome to stop by anytime your family is in the neighborhood."

Ashleigh felt a genuine smile tugging at the corners of her mouth. Mr. McPhearson would do what was best for Shadow. Mona was right—if anyone could get Shadow to the championship races, it was him. Ashleigh felt her heart lighten a little, knowing that Shadow was in the best of hands.

"Good-bye, girl." Ashleigh gave her one last pat and watched as Shadow loaded into the trailer. Ashleigh stood rooted to the spot until they had pulled down the driveway and driven out of sight.

Mr. Griffen put his hands on Ashleigh's shoulders and gave her a gentle squeeze. "I know this hurts, Ashleigh. But this is what our business is all about. You'll feel better about it someday when you see Shadow in the winner's circle with Mr. McPhearson. We're just part of the chain it takes to make a race-horse."

Mrs. Griffen offered an understanding smile. "It'll hurt for a few days, sweetheart. We've got to find something to take your mind off it. How about a party?" she suggested. "I was thinking we could invite the Gardners to our Thanksgiving Day meal. I'll let you be in charge of the decorations and the games. Would you like that?"

Ashleigh didn't feel like talking about parties at the moment, but she knew her mother was trying to help. She nodded and watched as her parents joined hands and walked back to the house.

"You going to be okay, Ash?" Caroline asked.

Ashleigh breathed a sorrowful sigh and turned back to the barn. "Yeah, I'll be okay. Thanks for asking, Caro." She trudged on toward the stable. There was no use telling her sister the truth—that her heart was badly damaged and might not ever get fixed.

"Was it awful?" Mona said when they met at her house an hour later.

Ashleigh just nodded. She felt numb from her riding helmet down to her boots. She didn't feel like talking right now. She just wanted to set her heels into Stardust's sides and feel the power of her mare eating up the ground beneath her. "Let's go for a good run," Ashleigh suggested.

Mona pointed Frisky down the driveway and out to the trails. "How much time do we have?"

Ashleigh glanced at her watch. "About an hour. We've got to go to the sale later. Three of our yearlings are running through today."

"Guess we better ride fast," Mona said with a grin.

They trotted the mares down the single-track trail until they got to the dirt road where it widened.

"Last one to the oak tree is a dirty muck rake!" Ashleigh called as she leaned low over Stardust's withers and asked the mare for everything she had.

Stardust responded immediately, stretching her neck as she grabbed for ground, her muscles expanding and contracting as she reached top speed. Ashleigh forgot everything in the world except beating Mona to the oak tree. Usually Frisky, a pure Thoroughbred, was the better racer, but not today. Ash-

61

leigh rode so fast, she left her troubles in the dirt the horses kicked out behind them.

"Hey, Ash, Slow down! The oak tree is way behind us!" Mona called as Stardust began to tire and Frisky pulled alongside the chestnut mare.

Ashleigh looked over at Mona in surprise, then at the scenery around them. She hadn't even noticed when they had passed the finish line.

"Jeez, Ash, you were really flying. We couldn't even catch you," Mona said between deep breaths. "You looked like a real jockey riding in the Kentucky Derby!"

Ashleigh smiled as she pulled Stardust down to a trot and then a walk. The ache in her heart still remained, but she felt a little better now. They turned the mares into the forest and rode toward the small pond to give the horses a drink. When they were watered, they took the long path on the other side of the forest toward home.

"Gee, look at all the mares and foals old man Potter has." Mona pointed toward a pasture full of horses.

Ashleigh really didn't feel like looking at foals at the moment, but she followed Mona as her friend rode closer to the big field. There were at least twenty mares and foals wandering around the pasture, trying to nibble what was left of the dry autumn grass.

"I wonder why he hasn't weaned any of them yet?"

Mona said. "Some of those foals look like they were first-of-the-year babies. They might be seven or eight months old now."

Ashleigh frowned. "The foals look pretty good, but his mares seem kind of skinny, don't you think?" She stared at the ribs that were beginning to show on many of the mares.

"Yeah, and he's got plenty of other pastures. Why is he keeping them all in this one dried-up field?" Mona said.

Ashleigh looked around. Something didn't seem right. But she wasn't sure what it was. Old Pop Potter usually took pretty good care of his horses. The old man always ran several head through the Keeneland sale at the same time Edgardale did. It was odd that he hadn't weaned any of his babies yet. Maybe he was trying something new this year?

Ashleigh glanced at her watch. "Come on, Mona. I've got to get home. My parents want to leave at three o'clock. I've got homework to get done before we leave."

They turned the mares and trotted for home. The rest of the Griffen family was getting ready for the sale when Ashleigh entered the house.

Elaine Griffen glanced at Ashleigh as she walked through the door. "I hope you're planning to take a bath?" she said as she eyed Ashleigh's dirty jeans.

"Remember, we're representing Edgardale. We've got to look presentable."

Ashleigh nodded as she ran up the stairs. "I'll be ready in twenty minutes," she promised. The homework would have to wait.

Caroline was still in the bathroom, curling her hair and putting on makeup, when Ashleigh pushed inside. She made a face. "The boys at the sale are there to look at the *horses*, Caroline. You could put on enough makeup to scare a clown, and they still wouldn't notice."

Caroline stuck out her tongue, then put her nose in the air. "That shows how much you know," she announced. "Not *all* of them are total horse nuts like you."

Ashleigh ignored her sister and climbed into the shower. The hot water felt good as it sprayed over her, washing away the dirt and horsehair.

"Don't take all day," Caroline warned as she put the final touches on her hair. "We're leaving in fifteen minutes."

Ashleigh made quick work of the shower, then dressed in her best jeans and a flowered shirt. She made it back downstairs just as everyone was ready to load up and go.

Lost in her thoughts of Shadow, Ashleigh didn't

think it took long before they were pulling onto Keeneland's beautiful grounds. She smiled as she stared out the window at the meticulously manicured lawns. Pines and oaks dotted the landscape, along with smaller trees that blossomed pink and white in the springtime.

The Keeneland yearling sale was one of the biggest and most prestigious horse auctions in the country. People came from all over the world to attend it. Ashleigh wondered if there would be any record-breaking bids today.

"Let's go check on our yearlings," Mr. Griffen said. "Then we'll go to the auction ring and see what kind of prices the horses are bringing today."

Jonas was grooming the Edgardale yearlings when they arrived. He had Bandit out in the aisle, and several potential buyers were admiring the large, light bay colt as Jonas ran a rub rag over him to bring out a brilliant shine.

"He's looking good," Mr. Griffen said. "How are the others doing?"

Jonas scratched his stubbled chin as he straightened and smiled at them. "They look fit for a king," he replied.

Mrs. Griffen walked into the stall of Marvey Mary's colt and put on his halter. "I hear there are several sultans here from the Arabian countries," she said. "And that same bunch of Japanese businessmen who paid all those millions for that son of Northern Dancer last year are back again."

Ashleigh's mind raced at the thought of having that kind of money to spend. She smiled just thinking about the sultans. She had heard that one of those rich men from Arabia had a racetrack set up in his backyard exactly like the track at Churchill Downs. He even imported the same dirt that they used at Churchill Downs so that everything would be identical to the Kentucky Derby track. Yet the winner's circle on Derby day had still eluded him.

"Let's go look at the horses," Rory said as he tugged on Ashleigh's arm.

"Go ahead." Mrs. Griffen waved them on. "Just be sure you're back in an hour. We want to get good seats for when our yearlings go through."

Ashleigh and Caroline each grabbed one of Rory's hands as they set off down the aisle. Rory was disgruntled, proudly proclaiming the fact that he knew how to act around horses, but the level of activity in the barn warranted extra caution. There were too many people and horses walking everywhere.

"Wow, look at *that* one!" Caroline stopped in her tracks.

Ashleigh knew that if a horse was spectacular enough for Caroline to notice it, it must be something pretty special. She peeked around the large groom who was standing in front of her, and her breath caught in her throat.

The large chestnut yearling with a blaze and two hind socks that stood there was spectacular. His handler trotted him down the aisle for a prospective buyer. There was a collective gasp from the onlookers as the colt arched his neck and put on a magnificent display.

"Let me have the catalog, Caro," Ashleigh said as she watched the colt trot back up the aisle toward them. She quickly thumbed through the pages, looking up his sale number. "Oh, he's by Tabasco Cat!" Ashleigh said with awe. "That stallion won the Preakness and Belmont when he was a three-year-old. This colt will probably go for a lot of money."

"Mark that page," Caroline said. "We'll be sure to watch for him."

They continued through the barn, looking at all the beautiful horses. Ashleigh dreamed about the day she would be able to attend the Keeneland sale and buy a racer of her own. She and Mona were going to have a full stable of racers.

"Come on, guys. We've got to get back," Caroline

said as she turned around, dragging everyone with her. "We've got five minutes until Mom and Dad want to go to the ring."

They returned to Edgardale's stalls. When Mr. and Mrs. Griffen were sure that Jonas had everything under control, they left to take their seats in the sale ring.

Ashleigh looked around the huge sales pavilion. There were all types of people, ranging from elegantly dressed men and women, to trainers and track men in their Sunday best, to grooms in their clean jeans, leaning against the walls while their yearlings passed through the sales ring. Ashleigh even caught a glimpse of the Arabian sultan that everyone was talking about.

For a while Ashleigh was able to take her mind off her problems and dull the pain she felt at Shadow's loss, but when the first Edgardale yearling took the stage, she felt the sadness return full force. They all sat on the edge of their seats as Bandit was led around the sale ring while bidders nodded or raised fingers to indicate they were raising the bid.

Ashleigh held her breath when she saw the sultan raise his jeweled hand to bid. She didn't want one of Edgardale's horses to go to a foreign country! The bidding continued to rise, and eventually the man dropped out of the competition. Ashleigh had no doubt that the sultan had all the money in the world to spend, but she knew that most buyers set a limit on what they were willing to pay for each horse. Fortunately, Bandit was going beyond what the man was willing to pay.

When the bidding finished, Bandit had brought over eighty thousand dollars! Ashleigh's parents were very happy with the price. The other two yearlings didn't do nearly as well, but they brought a respectable price and went to good racing farms. Her parents were satisfied with the sale.

After saying their final good-byes to the yearlings, everyone climbed into the car, exhausted. Ashleigh slept the entire way home, waking when they pulled into Edgardale's gravel driveway.

It was already past ten o'clock. As soon as all the horses were checked, everyone prepared for bed. While she was waiting for Caroline to get out of the bathroom, Ashleigh put on her pajamas, then picked up the sales catalog for the following day. As she flipped through the pages, she thought it was strange that Pop Potter didn't have any yearlings in the sale. The old man always sent at least six or seven yearlings to auction.

She thought back to the ride she and Mona had taken earlier that day. Something was going on at the

Potter place, but she couldn't quite put her finger on it.

Ashleigh closed the sale book and climbed into bed, but even after the lights had been turned out and her eyes were closed, she saw visions of the thin mares with their weanling-age foals still nursing. She made a mental note to talk to her parents about it in the morning. Something was definitely odd at the Potter place.

6

The rest of Edgardale's yearlings sold over the next couple of days. It was a busy week for Ashleigh. She got up early each morning and helped Jonas with the feeding, then went on to school. After school she hurried home to do her nightly chores before she attended the auction with her parents.

At first Ashleigh's parents had balked at letting her attend the sale on school nights, but Ashleigh had promised to take her homework with her and do it on the ride to and from the track and during lulls in the auction. So far she had been able to complete her work each day, but she fell into bed exhausted every night. That was okay with Ashleigh. The more tired she was, the less of an ache she felt at losing Shadow and all the yearlings.

By the time the auction ended, Edgardale had put in a respectable showing at the Keeneland sale. Bandit was the top-selling yearling in their barn, but the rest of the colts and fillies also sold for a decent price. Several of them went to well-known racing stables within the state. Slewette's filly went to Seattle, Washington, the original home of her grandfather, champion racehorse Seattle Slew.

As Ashleigh dragged herself onto the bus after school on Friday afternoon, she barely had the energy to smile at Mona. She sat down next to her friend and pushed her book bag under the seat in front of her, then leaned back and closed her eyes.

A soft tapping on the window drew her attention. Ashleigh looked out to see their friends Jamie and Lynne, smiling and waving.

"You guys going to the football game tomorrow night?" Jamie hollered through the glass.

Ashleigh pulled down the bus window. "I think my sister is, but I'm going to stay home and catch up on my sleep. It's been a tough week." She glanced at Mona. "Are you going?"

Mona shook her head. "I've got too much homework."

"Maybe next time," Jamie said as she tossed her long blond hair over her shoulders and waved good-bye.

"See you guys Monday." Lynne waved. "You take care, Ash."

Ashleigh settled back into her seat, feeling the weight of Mona's stare. "What?" she asked.

"Jamie and Lynne are worried about you," Mona said. "So am I, Ash. You're really taking Shadow's loss hard."

Ashleigh closed her eyes, leaning back into the uncomfortable seat. "It's just not fair that we never get to keep any of the foals." She could feel her eyes burning with unshed tears. She didn't want to cry like a baby in front of the other kids. "Let's just drop it, okay?"

"Okay." Mona shrugged.

They rode the rest of the way in silence. Ashleigh was so exhausted, she fell asleep, waking when Mona poked her on the arm.

"We're here, Ash. Don't forget your books." She stepped off the bus behind Ashleigh. "You probably want to catch up on your sleep today, but how about if tomorrow we ride out and look at Pop Potter's horses?"

Ashleigh nodded as she slung her book bag over her shoulder and trudged toward the house. All she wanted to do at the moment was fall asleep and forget that this week had ever existed.

•   •   •

Ashleigh woke bright and early on Saturday morning. She had gone to bed right after supper the night before. She finally felt rested, but there was still a dull ache in the area of her heart.

Without waking Caroline, she got out of bed and dressed for a ride. Ashleigh actually felt a smile forming on her lips as she thought about taking a canter on Stardust with Mona and Frisky. It had been such a busy week, she hadn't ridden at all.

"Well, aren't you the early bird," Mrs. Griffen said as she sat at the kitchen table, sipping her morning coffee. "There's some Danish on the counter if you're just looking for a quick bite."

Ashleigh poured herself a big glass of milk and chose the roll with the cherry filling and sugar glaze. She took the chair next to her mother and bit into the Danish, laughing when the sticky filling dripped down her chin.

Mrs. Griffen offered her a napkin. "I should have warned you they're extra gooey." She reached out to wipe some crumbs from Ashleigh's cheek. "So what has you up and about so early?"

Ashleigh took a big gulp of milk. "I thought I'd help put the mares out, then Mona and I were planning to go for a ride. We thought we'd ride over and check out those broodmares I was telling you about."

"That sounds like a good plan," Mrs. Griffen said.

"I'm sure that by now, Mr. Potter will have weaned those foals. Let me grab my work boots, and I'll walk out to the barn with you."

When they got to the barn, Derek Griffen and Jonas were just finishing with the last of the grain buckets.

"The first mares should be ready to go out to pasture," Mr. Griffen said. "Wanderer and Go Gen were the last two fed."

Ashleigh picked up a carrot and went to see Stardust. The mare had just finished licking her bucket clean and eagerly stepped forward to see what treat Ashleigh had to offer. "You're such a gobble gut." Ashleigh giggled, thinking that the past week had been filled with so much crying that it felt good to laugh again.

She saw her parents look at each other and smile. In that moment she realized how much they had been worried about her. Had she really been that bad? She made a mental note to try smiling a little more when she was around them—even if she did still hurt every time she looked at all the empty stalls from the missing horses.

Ashleigh pulled a halter off the wall and entered Slewette's stall. "Let's go, big girl," she said as she buckled the halter around the bay mare's head.

When all of the broodmares were out to pasture, Ashleigh led Stardust into the aisle and hooked her into the crossties. The chestnut mare snorted and bobbed her head.

"I know," Ashleigh said as she ran a quieting hand down the mare's neck. "It's been days since you've been ridden, and you're ready to go." As she told Stardust about the coming ride to old man Potter's place, she felt her excitement growing. Would the babies be weaned yet?

Again she cautioned herself against getting too involved. She had promised not to get so wound up in young horses again. And these weren't even hers!

Ashleigh tacked her mare, then made a final check of her equipment before riding out to meet Mona. It felt good to be back on her horse again.

Mona and Frisky were waiting by the old oak tree when Ashleigh and her horse topped the rise. It was early October, and most of the beautifully colored leaves were pooled at the base of the tree. So far the weather had held, but it wouldn't be long before the rain and snow came, making the land look bleak and desolate. The horses were already getting furry with winter coats.

Ashleigh smiled and waved as she approached. "I've got all day until chore time before I have to be back. Let's go!"

They cantered across the field and entered the forest, following the well-known single-track path that would take them through the woods. They slowed the horses to a walk to avoid the danger of several low-hanging branches.

"Are you still going to the big Halloween party that Jamie is having?" Mona asked.

"Sure," Ashleigh said as she turned in the saddle to give Mona a questioning stare. "Why wouldn't I?"

Mona shrugged. "You've just been so bummed out lately, I thought that maybe you didn't want to attend any of the holiday parties."

Ashleigh pressed her lips together in a frown. "I'm sorry I haven't been very good company lately," she apologized. "So much has happened in the last couple of weeks. I really miss Shadow and all the yearlings."

Mona nodded in understanding. "I don't know how you do it, Ash. I couldn't stand having to say good-bye to so many horses."

Ashleigh reached out to pull a dried leaf from a branch. It crumpled in her hand, floating away on the breeze in several broken pieces. That was how her heart felt at the moment. She was sure it was scattered in several pieces within her chest.

"Most of the time it's not so bad," Ashleigh said. "We know our yearlings are going to good homes, and we'll get to see many of them race." She paused and drew a deep breath. "It was just different this year because of Shadow."

Mona rode up beside Ashleigh as they exited the forest trails. "I think you got really attached to her because you were there when she was born," Mona said. "You guys formed a special bond. That's what made it so hard to let go this time."

Ashleigh pressed her lips together in a grim line. "That's why from now on, I'm not getting too close to any of the foals."

Mona looked incredulous. "Come on, Ash. You don't mean that."

"Yes, I do," Ashleigh said with determination. "I'm staying out of the foaling barn next year. They're all just going to be sold, anyway, so there's no used getting attached to them. I'll just stick to Stardust and the broodmares. My parents won't sell any of them."

Mona huffed. "That's totally unreal, Ashleigh. You live on a breeding farm. There are horses everywhere! And think of all the fun you have with those babies. Isn't it worth putting up with a little bit of sadness when they have to leave?"

Ashleigh's head snapped around. "This isn't *a little bit of sadness,*" she growled. "Shadow meant a lot to me! I hate walking out to the pasture and knowing that she's not going to whinny and come running."

Mona shook her head. "I've told you this before, Ash. Horses are in your blood. You'll be miserable if you can't play with the foals and yearlings. Sometimes we have to enjoy the good things we have, even when we know they're not going to last forever. Think of all the good memories you have so far."

Ashleigh stared straight ahead, keeping her eyes on the trail. She rocked to the lazy four-beat rhythm of Stardust's walk as they rode in silence. Part of her knew that Mona was right. Horses were her life. But she couldn't bear going through another separation like she had with Shadow. "Can we change the subject?" she asked.

"Sure," Mona agreed. "Let's talk about the party and all the fun things we're going to do with the holidays coming up."

Ashleigh bumped Stardust into a trot. "It's going to be great having your family over for Thanksgiving this year."

"Yeah, can you believe they're actually going to trust us to bake the pies!" Mona laughed.

Ashleigh felt some warmth flooding back into her heart. It had been a horrible couple of weeks, and she wasn't sure what she was going to do to make things better with the horses, but it sure helped having a friend like Mona. "Have you decided what you're going to wear to the costume party?" Ashleigh asked.

"My mom's making me this really cool costume!" Mona said. "It's like those fancy outfits those Cossack horsemen wore when we saw that Russian circus act on television."

"Wow! Your mom is really good at sewing. Those were really pretty costumes." Ashleigh smiled. "Looks like we'll have the same theme . . . horses! I was going to have it be a surprise, but Rhoda sent me some of her old jockey silks. I'm going to the party as a jockey!"

Mona pressed Frisky into a lope as they hit the wide part of the trail. "What else?" She laughed. "I should have suspected as much. This is going to be a really cool party. Lynne is going to make up a horse race game, and Jamie's dad has promised to call the race."

"That'll be so cool," Ashleigh said. "He calls the races at Churchill Downs. We can have our own Kentucky Derby!"

They came to the edge of Potter's property. They slowed the horses and stopped at the back fence line.

"I don't believe it," Ashleigh said as she stared at the pasture full of mares and foals. "They're all still here."

Mona walked Frisky farther down the fence to get a better view. "And look at them," she said in alarm. "The mares look awful! All their ribs are showing."

Ashleigh dismounted and tied Stardust to a post. "The foals aren't quite as bad as their mothers, but they look pretty skinny, too." She climbed the fence and dropped to the other side, taking in the dried, overcropped grass that didn't look like it could support a single horse, let alone all of these mares and foals.

"What are you doing, Ash?" Mona dismounted, but she stayed on her own side of the fence.

Ashleigh waved her forward. "Come on, Mona. We've got to see what's going on here. Something isn't right. Mr. Potter always takes good care of his horses. These mares look like they haven't been off this pasture since the last time we saw them. And I don't think he's been throwing them any hay, either."

Ashleigh walked across the dry, brittle pasture toward a bay mare and her large foal. She fumbled in her pocket for the carrots she had brought along for Stardust and Frisky. They wouldn't mind missing out on their treat if it meant helping the other horses.

"Look at her," Mona said in concern as she came to join Ashleigh. "I can count every single one of her ribs."

The big bay mare lifted her head and snorted as Mona and Ashleigh approached.

"Easy, baby," Ashleigh crooned. "Come here, sweetie —I've got something for you."

The mare's nostrils quivered as she breathed in their scent. She picked up the smell of the carrots and blew through her lips as she walked cautiously forward, extending her neck to reach for Ashleigh's outstretched hand. She snapped up the carrots and greedily crunched them, nuzzling Ashleigh's hand for more.

Some of the nearby mares saw that the bay mare was eating and came to see if there was something for them. They pushed forward, trying to get close to the girls.

"Careful, Ash," Mona warned. "If they start a fight, we'll be right in the middle of it."

A large chestnut mare trotted up, nipping the flanks of the other mares and foals as she pushed and bullied her way through the crowd. The bay mare Ashleigh had been feeding panicked and bolted out of the way, bumping Ashleigh hard as she went.

"We better get out of here before we get stampeded," Ashleigh said as she grabbed Mona's hand and ran for the fence. She began to panic when she heard the sound of several horses running behind them.

"Hurry, Ash!" Mona cried. "They're all coming!"

They reached the fence and jumped for the top, scrambling over the boards as the mares slid to a halt on the other side.

"Boy, they must really be hungry to chase us like that," Mona said as she wiped the sweat from her brow. "What are we going to do? Should we go home and get some hay?"

Ashleigh shook her head. "No, we couldn't carry

enough hay back here on Stardust and Frisky to feed them all. I think we should go home and tell my parents. They'll know what to do. Maybe they can go see old man Potter and find out what's wrong."

Several of the mares stretched their heads over the fence and nickered. Their eyes seemed so hopeful.

Ashleigh bent down to pull a handful of grass. There was still plenty of it on this side of the fence. It was turning brown, but it had grown high along the trail. "Let's pick a bunch of this and throw it over the fence for them," she suggested. "It isn't much, but it's more than they have in their field."

The girls set to work, picking every blade of grass on their side of the divider and throwing it over the fence. The hungry mares snatched it up, munching happily on the haylike dried grasses.

"Look at that one." Mona pointed to a small pale-gray mare. The mare stood at the back of the herd, snatching up any stray blade of food she could get.

"Wow, she looks like she's ready to foal any time," Ashleigh said. "But it's way too late in the season. Our last foal was born in May."

"Maybe it's this year's foal, and she's just really big," Mona said as she held out a bunch of grass, trying to coax the mare closer to the fence.

Ashleigh looked at the mare between the boards of the fence. "I don't think so. The other mares aren't this big. See how her belly is kind of moving back and she's starting to droop around her upper flank? She looks like she's going to foal in a month or so."

Ashleigh smiled as the little gray mare inched forward, trying to escape the notice of the other mares. She stretched her neck toward the fence and quickly snatched the blades of grass from Ashleigh's hand. But the large chestnut noticed her and made a teeth-baring dive at her haunches.

Ashleigh winced at the sound of hoof on muscle as the chestnut wheeled on the little gray mare and let fly with a warning kick. "You get out of here!" she screamed at the bullying mare. Ashleigh knew it was the way of horses to have a pecking order, but the small gray mare was the worst-looking one of the bunch. Despite her swollen belly, every rib stuck out in sharp contrast. She was a sore sight in the middle of a herd of sorry-looking horses.

Ashleigh felt a tug at her heart, but she ignored it. She was *not* going to get involved in another no-win situation. This mare belonged to somebody else. She would ride home and tell her parents about these poor mares and foals. They would know what to do. Ashleigh didn't need to get her heart trampled on again. "Let's go home and tell my parents," she said as she gathered Stardust's reins and mounted up.

They trotted toward Edgardale, not daring to push

the horses any faster on the single-track path through the forest.

Mona waved when they parted company at the front gate. "Call me after supper and let me know what happened."

Ashleigh nodded, then pointed Stardust toward the barn. She hooked the mare into the crossties and removed her tack. "Have you seen my parents?" she asked Jonas as the old stable hand exited the tack room with an armload of things to clean.

Jonas tipped his head toward the back of the barn. "They're out with the weanlings," he muttered. "It's worming time."

Ashleigh quickly brushed the dried sweat from Stardust's coat, then put her out to pasture before going to find her parents. She looked across the fields of Edgardale as she walked to the weanlings' pen. Edgardale's fields were also brown with the coming of winter, but they didn't look anything like the barren pasture the mares and foals were in. Potter's field looked like a herd of starving sheep had moved through it, eating everything down to the bare root.

She found her parents and told them about how bad the mares looked. "I know something is wrong over there," Ashleigh said. "Mr. Potter didn't run any of his horses through the sale this year, either. He always sends something to Keeneland."

Mrs. Griffen gave her husband a worried frown. "Ashleigh may be on to something," she agreed as she slipped the halter from Althea's foal and prepared a syringe of wormer for the colt her husband was holding. "I remember hearing that old Pop wasn't feeling very well last month. I hope the old guy is all right."

Derek Griffen grunted as the colt he was holding lunged forward, stomping on his feet as he tried to escape his hold. "Argh!" he growled, holding the colt still until the wormer was administered. He turned the fussing colt loose and rubbed his instep. "I've got to go over that way tomorrow. I'll drop in and pay Mr. Potter a visit."

Ashleigh helped with the remainder of the worming, then they retired to the house for a small snack break before evening chores. That night after dinner Ashleigh sat in the window seat in her bedroom, looking through photos of the sale yearlings and the few pictures she had of Shadow. The melancholy ache that had followed her all week returned.

She hated this feeling—like there was a big, empty hole inside her. She thought about the upcoming Halloween party and Thanksgiving with the Gardners. The hole began to feel like it was being filled in.

The phone sounded downstairs as Ashleigh put down the horse pictures and picked up the framed portrait of her and Mona at last summer's jump show. She smiled. Someday she and Mona were going to be running their own farms. They'd raise the best racehorses in Kentucky, and they'd take turns winning the Derby! They'd definitely be best friends forever!

"Ashleigh?" Caroline peeked her head into the room, making a face at all the mess on Ashleigh's side of it. "Mona's on the phone. She sounds kind of upset."

Ashleigh put down the portrait and went to answer the phone. "Hey, Mona," she said into the receiver. "What's up?" There was a long, silent pause on the line. Ashleigh was just about to see if she'd been disconnected when she heard a heart-wrenching sob. "Mona? What's the matter?" She felt the hairs on the back of her neck stand on end. Something was terribly wrong.

"Ashleigh . . ." Mona hiccuped as she tried to get the words out. "Ashleigh, my father got a promotion. We're moving to California. . . ."

7

Ashleigh stood there with the phone in her hand and a million thoughts tumbling through her head. This couldn't be true! *Mona would never move from here and leave me,* her mind screamed. It had to be a joke, Ashleigh thought. But she knew Mona would never kid about anything like this.

"Ashleigh? Are you there?" Mona said between sniffs.

Ashleigh stood silent. She didn't know what to say. She opened her mouth to speak, but nothing came out.

"Ashleigh?"

"I—I'm here," Ashleigh stammered. She took a deep breath, feeling the room begin to spin around her. "Wh-When?" was all she could manage to say.

"I'm not sure," Mona said, her voice full of tears. "My dad's flying out to Los Angeles on Monday. He's going to look for a place for us to live."

Los Angeles! Monday! Ashleigh felt like the wind had been knocked out of her. She gulped for air, but it didn't seem like there was enough to fill her lungs.

Caroline looked up from the magazine she was reading at the kitchen table. "Are you all right, Ash? You don't look so good."

Ashleigh sat down hard on the wooden chair that was positioned by the phone. This was too cruel. She still felt the loss of the yearlings. And with all the pain she had suffered at losing Shadow, this was too much! It was bad enough to miss the horses, but she couldn't lose her best friend. *She just couldn't!*

"How long will it take him to find a place to live?" Ashleigh finally managed to speak a whole sentence.

"I don't know." Mona took a deep breath and choked back another sob. "We're putting our house up for sale on Monday. I guess my mother and I are going to stay here until the farm is sold, then we'll move to L.A. with my dad. I'm going to miss you so much, Ash!"

Not live next to Mona? Ashleigh's mind reeled. What about all their plans? What about all the foals they were going to raise together and race? "I can't believe this!" Ashleigh cried. "This isn't happening! What about the Halloween party in a couple of weeks? What about all the holidays that we were going to spend together? You can't leave!" A flood of tears clouded her eyes. Her throat felt like it was closing up, and no more words would come out. A sob tore loose from her throat, and her heart felt like it was being squeezed from her chest.

"*Mommmm!*" Rory yelled as he came into the kitchen and noticed his sister's distress. "Come quick! Ashleigh needs help!"

Ashleigh gasped for breath, motioning for Rory to come to her. She didn't want him to be upset. She hugged her little brother close. The telephone was still clutched in her hand. "I'm okay," she said to Rory, even though she knew she wasn't. At that moment it felt like *nothing* was ever going to be okay again.

"Ashleigh, what's the matter?" Mrs. Griffen ran into the room, kneeling beside the chair to pry Rory off Ashleigh. "Who's on the phone, honey?"

She mouthed the word *Mona,* then spoke into the receiver. "I'm so sorry, Mona. I can't believe any of this. This can't be real. I feel like I'm in a nightmare. Can you go with us tomorrow to Mr. Potter's place?" She looked pleadingly at her mother.

Mrs. Griffen nodded as she brushed a strand of dark hair behind Ashleigh's ear. "I'm sure your father will be more than happy to take you both," she said.

"We can talk more tomorrow," Ashleigh said. "I'm so confused right now, I don't know what to say. I'll see you tomorrow morning."

Ashleigh hung up the phone, feeling totally dead inside. She told her family about Mona having to move. What was she going to do without Mona? After several sympathetic stares from her family, Ashleigh decided to pay a visit to the barn. Maybe a talk with Stardust would help her feel better. She pulled on her boots and let herself out into the night.

There were several questioning nickers when Ashleigh opened the barn door. She could hear the muffled wail of country music coming from Jonas's small apartment, but she doubted if he would come out. The horses had already been tucked in for the night.

Ashleigh walked down the barn aisle, trying to convince herself that everything was going to turn out okay, but all of the empty yearling stalls only served to remind her of the huge loss. She looked at Shadow's blue halter hanging on the wall, and another pain pummeled her heart.

Stardust nickered again, and Ashleigh went to the tack room to get some carrots. As she reached for the package, something slipped from the desk and fell to the floor. Ashleigh bent to retrieve the dropped item, noting that it was a pair of Mona's leather riding gloves that she must have forgotten to take home.

Ashleigh lifted them to her nose, breathing in the scent of leather and horses. That was the smell she and Mona liked best in all the world. A tear trickled down Ashleigh's cheek and fell on the gloves, leaving a dark stain on the leather. It was quickly followed by another. What was she going to do without Mona?

Stardust whinnied, drawing Ashleigh's attention. She wiped her tears, then grabbed several carrots and a brush and went to the mare's stall. Ashleigh broke the carrots into pieces, feeding them to Stardust as she talked to her about the horrible phone call from Mona.

Stardust flicked her ears back and forth, seeming to pay close attention to all Ashleigh had to say. Ashleigh picked up the body brush and continued to talk while she ran the grooming tool over the mare's gleaming copper coat.

"You understand, don't you, girl?" Ashleigh said as she tossed the brush into a corner and threw her arms around Stardust's neck. "You'll never leave me, will you?"

Stardust stood patiently while Ashleigh cried into her silky mane. Even when Ashleigh was all cried out, the pain was still there. She wondered if it would ever go away.

She heard the creak of the barn door and rubbed her hand over her eyes, trying to clear her blurry vision. Footfalls sounded down the barn aisle. They stopped in front of Stardust's stall, but Ashleigh's eyes were so swollen, she couldn't see who it was in the dim light.

"I thought I might find you here." Mrs. Griffen's voice echoed gently from outside the stall. She opened the door and drew Ashleigh into her arms, hugging her tightly. "I wish I could tell you that everything was going to be all right, Ashleigh, but it's never all right when you lose a friend." She gave Ashleigh a Kleenex and led her out of the stall. "Especially a great friend like Mona."

Ashleigh nodded as she allowed herself to be led back to the house. "Why does she have to go?" Ashleigh said as she sniffed and blew her nose.

Mrs. Griffen steered Ashleigh up the front porch steps. "Sometimes kids get caught up in the decisions that their parents make. Mona's father was offered a high-paying job in California. But it's not the other side of the world, Ashleigh," Mrs. Griffen said as she opened the screen door and followed her daughter inside. "You can always go visit."

Ashleigh looked at the rest of her family as they sat in the living room, staring at her with anxious faces. "But it won't be the same," she said, hanging her head.

Mr. Griffen put a comforting hand on Ashleigh's shoulder. "I'm sorry this had to happen, honey. Losing a best friend is tough. My advice is to enjoy the time you have left. Mona's hurting just as badly as you, and she needs your friendship to help her through this.

Imagine how scared she is," Mr. Griffen said. "She's got to deal with a new home and a new school."

Ashleigh wiped her eyes. She wished she could see Mona right now, but it was almost bedtime. She'd have to wait until the morning. She went to her room and changed into her pajamas, her movements feeling stiff and mechanical. She climbed into bed, too exhausted to even turn out the light.

"Ashleigh . . ." Mrs. Griffen poked her head into the room. "Your father will be ready to go in about twenty minutes. You better get up and get ready."

Ashleigh heard her mother's voice like it was coming through a thick fog. She fought to open her eyes, squinting at the clock. She was shocked to see it was almost nine-thirty. She never slept this late! As she threw her legs over the side of the bed, she heard her sister's voice.

"How do you feel this morning, Ash?" Caroline handed her a glass of orange juice and a slice of toast.

"Fine," she said as she accepted the quick breakfast. But the truth was, she didn't feel fine. She felt like she had been run over by a herd of rampaging horses. She felt sluggish and disoriented. She hadn't realized crying would take so much out of her.

Mona was waiting in the kitchen when Ashleigh came downstairs. She felt the smile immediately come to her face. It soon turned to a frown when she took in Mona's puffy eyes and red nose. "Oh, oh," Ashleigh said. "Do I look as bad as you do?"

Both girls erupted into peals of laughter.

"Good thing we're best friends, or I'd be *really* insulted!" Mona giggled.

Ashleigh smiled as they followed her father out the door. She knew it wouldn't last long, but for now, her world seemed right once more.

They loaded into the old pickup and drove the short couple of miles to Pop Potter's farm. Ashleigh had an uncomfortable feeling when they pulled into the driveway and saw the overgrown grass and scattered garbage cans. Something wasn't right.

"You girls wait here while I go to the door," Mr. Griffen said. "I want to make sure everything is okay."

They watched as Derek Griffen walked to the front door and rang the doorbell. He waited several moments, then rang it again.

"What do you suppose is the matter?" Mona said.

Ashleigh pressed her nose against the window, staring at the buildup of leaves on the old man's lawn. "It doesn't look like anybody is even living here right now," she observed. She watched as her father went to the front window of the house and cupped his hands on the glass to peek inside. He returned to the door with a frown on his face and tested the knob.

Ashleigh gasped as the door pushed inward and her father disappeared inside. After several minutes she began to worry. "Maybe we should go see what he's doing," she said to Mona.

Mona kept her eyes on the front door. "I don't know, Ash—he told us to wait in the car."

Ashleigh had her hand on the truck's door handle and was considering going in just when her father exited the house.

"Mr. Potter is awfully sick," Mr. Griffen said. "I think maybe he's had a stroke. I called the ambulance and his son. I'll wait inside with him until the ambulance arrives."

Within a few minutes the wail of a siren could be heard in the distance. "Wow," Ashleigh said. "No wonder his horses weren't being taken care of."

Ashleigh and Mona waited while Mr. Griffen helped the ambulance drivers with Mr. Potter. Soon the ambulance pulled out of the driveway and sped into the distance.

Mr. Griffen returned to the truck. He ran a worried hand through his hair. "Whatever is wrong with Mr. Potter, I think it must have affected his ability to think. He was somewhat taking care of himself these last couple of weeks, but I think he forgot he had horses to care for. He's a stubborn old man," Mr. Griffen said. "He didn't want to call anyone for help."

"What will happen to all of the horses?" Ashleigh asked.

"I told Mr. Potter's son we'd feed the mares and foals and get them moved off that skimpy pasture," Mr. Griffen said. "You girls feel up to doing a little work?"

Ashleigh and Mona nodded eagerly. They scrambled out of the truck and followed Mr. Griffen to the back pasture, opening a series of gates that would move the mares into a field closer to the barn. They got out the wheelbarrow and hauled several bales of hay to the mares.

Ashleigh noticed the little gray mare that was heavy with foal. She was moving very slowly. Ashleigh hoped she would be all right.

Once the mares and foals were taken care of, they headed for home. Ashleigh spent the remainder of the day with Mona. For a while it felt just like old times, but when it was time to say good-bye, Ashleigh was suddenly reminded that someday soon, she would be saying good-bye for good.

8

The days got more and more difficult for Ashleigh. Every morning she woke with the feeling that *this* could be the day Mona's house sold and her friend would be torn from her life forever.

Ashleigh stared out the window as she readied herself for school. She felt as empty inside as those barren trees that swayed with the cold, late October winds. She turned from the window and reached for her good school jeans. The photo of her and Mona at the jumping show confronted her.

Ashleigh sighed. Everywhere she went, she was reminded of her losses. When she went to visit Stardust, all she saw were the rows of empty stalls where the yearlings and Shadow had been. When she got on the school bus, it passed in front of Mona's house, where the big yellow For Sale sign was planted on her front lawn. It seemed like every time Ashleigh turned around, she hurt.

Everyone was being really nice to her. Her friends and family did everything they could to cheer her up, but nothing worked. Ashleigh knew the pain would eventually fade, but until it did, she felt awful! She never wanted to be this sad again.

Caroline burst into the room. "Where's my purse?" She looked at Ashleigh, still dressed in her pajamas, and frowned. "You better hurry up, Ash. The bus will be here in ten minutes. You haven't eaten, you're not dressed, and you haven't even visited the horses yet. You better get with it, or you'll miss the bus." She found her purse under a pile of Ashleigh's clothes. "And clean up your half of the room!" she said before storming out the door.

Ashleigh stuck out her tongue at her sister's retreating form. She glanced around the room at the piles of clothing. It looked like a dirty-laundry bomb had exploded in her half of the bedroom.

Horse magazines lay scattered around the floor. She felt a pang of guilt as she reached out to pick up a recent issue of her favorite equine magazine. She hadn't turned past the cover. Now she opened it to the middle to see this month's poster. She frowned as she stared at the mare and foal caught in a beautiful pose.

Ashleigh quickly snapped the publication closed. She didn't even want to look at the photo. She hated this feeling of being torn up inside. She didn't *ever* want to feel like this again. She tossed the magazine aside and reached for her school clothes. She had five minutes left to catch the bus.

"I'm leaving, Ash," Caroline hollered from the bottom of the stairs. "You better not miss the bus!"

Ashleigh thought about Mona waiting for her at the bus stop. Would this be the morning she'd deliver the bad news? She grabbed her book bag and tossed it over her shoulder. Three minutes until the bus would arrive. Ashleigh took her time going downstairs. She visited the kitchen and popped a couple of toaster pastries into the toaster.

Several minutes later she heard the roar of the old school bus's engine as it chugged up the hill, then screeched to a halt to load everyone up. Ashleigh took a bite of her breakfast and listened as the engine's whine receded into the distance. When she was finished with her breakfast, she went to the barn to find her parents.

"Ashleigh?" Mrs. Griffen straightened from the hay net she was filling and tucked a lock of stray blond hair back under her hat. "Did you miss the bus again?"

Ashleigh nodded. Her mother didn't look very happy.

"Derek," Mrs. Griffen hollered down the barn aisle. "I've got to take Ashleigh to school."

Derek Griffen poked his head out from the stall he was cleaning. "Again?" He looked at Ashleigh and frowned. "This is getting to be a habit, Ashleigh. I don't know what's gotten into you lately." He scratched his head. "I like the fact that you're studying more and your grades are improving, but you're slacking off around the barn, and this missing-the-bus routine has got to stop. Your mother and I are very busy, especially since we've been having to pick up a lot of your chores."

Ashleigh kicked at the stray pieces of straw that littered the barn aisle. She hated being scolded. But she knew she deserved it. She had purposely missed the bus this morning, and she hadn't been spending much time around the barn. Stardust poked her head over her stall and whinnied so hard, her body shook. Ashleigh stared guiltily at the ground.

"Your Halloween party is tomorrow night," Mr. Griffen said with a note of warning in his voice. "Make sure you get right home and get your stalls cleaned tonight, or we may have to rethink letting you go to that."

Ashleigh nodded and followed her mother out to the car.

"Honestly, Ashleigh," Mrs. Griffen said as she turned the key and the car roared to life. "This *new you* has me a bit worried. Caroline tells me you've joined the Pep Squad, and you're starting to hang out with different kids at school."

"Can't I have new friends?" Ashleigh said.

Mrs. Griffen sighed. "Yes, honey. New friends are good, but just make sure it's not at the expense of your old friends. It seems to me like you're running away from your problems."

Ashleigh stared out the car window at the bleak landscape as they drove toward the school. The oaks and maples that had been so colorful only weeks ago now stood barren in the brown fields. She felt like the landscape was a refection of her life at the moment.

The big party they had all been waiting for was tomorrow night, and she wasn't even excited. Jamie and Lynne had been making decorations for weeks. They had invited Mona and Ashleigh over for several preparation parties, but Ashleigh had always declined, saying that she had too much homework. The next day at school Mona would tell her of all the fun they had.

"Here we are," Mrs. Griffen said as she pulled in front of the school. She reached out to touch Ashleigh's cheek. "I know you're going through a really rough time right now, honey, but things will get better. The holidays are coming up, and you've got your big Halloween party that you've been looking forward to for so long. You and Mona will have a great time."

Ashleigh kissed her mother on the cheek and got out of the car. She'd see Mona at lunchtime and make plans for going to the party. Maybe if they started talking about all the fun they were going to have, she'd feel more like going.

The morning passed slowly. Ashleigh had classes with Jamie and Lynne. They were excited about the coming party.

"We got these really cool horse costumes!" Jamie said between classes as they walked down the hall. "Wait until you see them."

"Yeah," Lynne piped up. "I'm going as my Welsh pony, and Jamie is going as that chestnut jump mare she wants her parents to buy her."

Ashleigh had to smile. The party did sound like fun. Everyone was looking forward to it.

"What are you wearing, Ash?" Jamie asked.

Ashleigh grinned, her mood feeling lighter already. "You'll just have to wait and see. All I can tell you is, it sounds like my costume will fit right in."

She met Mona for lunch. They sat at a table with Jamie and Lynne and pulled out their sack lunches.

School lunch was so gross, they only ate the hot meal when it was hamburgers or pizza.

"What's that?" Mona asked as she pointed at Ashleigh's hands.

Ashleigh shrugged as she stuck her hands under the table, feeling the color rise in her cheeks.

"What is it, Ash?" Jamie pushed her long blond hair over her shoulders and stared at her curiously.

"Come on, what are you hiding?" Lynne reached for Ashleigh's hands and pulled them on top of the table, turning them over and studying them closely.

"I don't see anything," Jamie said.

Mona scrunched her lips. "You're wearing nail polish, Ash. Since when did you start wearing nail polish?"

Ashleigh scowled at Mona. "It's nothing," she grouched. "Caroline wanted to try out a new color on me, that's all." She grabbed her tuna sandwich and took a big bite, trying to act like it was no big deal.

"But you never wore nail polish before. No matter *how much* Caroline bugged you," Mona said accusingly.

"Oh, lay off it, Mona!" Jamie huffed. "If Ashleigh wants to wear nail polish, what's the difference?"

But Ashleigh saw the look in Mona's eyes. Mona *knew* there was a difference. She finished her lunch as quickly as possible, listening to the conversation but not doing much of the talking.

The rest of the school day passed at a snail's pace, but eventually they were on the school bus, heading for home.

"You want to go for a ride?" Mona asked hopefully.

Ashleigh shook her head. "I can't. I've got to do a lot of barn chores, or my parents won't let me go to the party tomorrow."

Mona sighed in disappointment. "Poor Stardust hasn't been getting much exercise lately."

Ashleigh stared out the window at the fields of horses and cows. Mona was right about that. Ashleigh had barely ridden Stardust in the past couple of weeks. Mona's voice pulled at Ashleigh's wandering mind.

"Have I done something to upset you, Ash?" Mona grabbed her backpack and prepared to exit at their bus stop. "You haven't been over to my house or been riding with me in a long time. If I've done something to make you mad, please tell me. We don't have a lot of time left together. I don't want to waste what little time we have left."

Ashleigh picked at her fingernail polish, feeling guilty. Everything Mona said was true. She *did* want to spend more time with Mona, but every time she did, she thought about her friend living on the other side of the country and it hurt. "No, you haven't done anything," Ashleigh said. "I've just been really busy with homework and stuff." She smiled at Mona. "We'll go to the Halloween party tomorrow and have a really good time."

"Great!" Mona said as they hopped off the bus, and she waved to Ashleigh. "We'll pick you up at six o'clock tomorrow night."

Ashleigh ran to the house and quickly changed into her barn clothes. She was a little more excited about going to the party. She was going to get to wear her jockey costume! And it was a real one!

When she entered the stable yard, she noticed Jonas was hooking up the horse trailer. Her heart began to pound. Her parents weren't selling another one of Edgardale's horses, were they? She ran into the barn, searching frantically for Stardust. They wouldn't sell her horse, would they?

Stardust wasn't in her stall. Ashleigh knew her thoughts were irrational, but crazy things had been happening lately. She didn't trust fate not to take away her last prized possession. She ran out of the barn and called across the pasture, "Stardust!"

She paused, listening for an answering call, but all she heard was the nicker of the nearest broodmare. Ashleigh pulled her collar up against the cool breeze and ran to the other side of the barn. "Staarrr . . ." She stopped short when she saw the copper head with the irregular blaze pop over the fence and whinny.

"Stardust!" Ashleigh cried as she ran to the fence and threw her arms around the mare's neck.

"What's going on, Ashleigh?" Mr. Griffen said as he walked from the weanling pen with Slewette's bay filly.

"I saw Jonas hooking up the horse trailer, and I couldn't find Stardust. . . ." She hugged her mare, running her hand down the white blaze on her face.

"Ashleigh," Mr. Griffen said in dismay. "We wouldn't sell your mare. Every horse that's been sold on Edgardale is one of the babies that we had every intention of selling from the beginning. You know that."

Ashleigh had the good grace to feel ashamed. What her father said was true. Her parents would never sell her horse out from under her. She didn't know what had come over her. She'd been so mixed up lately. "I'm sorry, Dad. I just panicked." She scratched Stardust behind the ears. Maybe she'd take her for a ride tomorrow before the party. "But why is Jonas hooking up the trailer?"

Mr. Griffen tied the bay weanling to a hitching post and bent to inspect a scrape on the filly's front leg. "Mr. Potter's son has asked me to haul a couple of horses to the sale for him. The old man won't be able to care for all those mares and foals, so he's running a bunch of them through the Keeneland breeding stock sale next week."

Mr. Griffen straightened and untied the filly. "Your

mother and I were thinking about taking some of the money we made on the yearlings and buying another broodmare. There are a couple of mares in the sale that look pretty good. Are you interested in going to the sale?"

Ashleigh shook her head. "I promised Caroline I'd go to the football game with her next Saturday." She turned her head, not wanting to look her father in the eye. She knew what she'd see there—disbelief. She left her father with the filly and went to the barn to do her chores.

I shouldn't feel guilty, she told herself. What was the point of going to the sale and buying another broodmare? She'd just have another baby that they'd be getting rid of. Ashleigh got out the wheelbarrow and pitchfork and set to work. She had just twenty-four more hours until she'd be getting ready for the Halloween party.

Ashleigh stared at herself in the mirror. She couldn't believe her eyes. She fingered the cool, slippery nylon of the bright red jockey silks.

"Whoa!" Rory said when he walked into the bedroom. "You look like a real jockey, Ash. That's really cool! Can I try them on?"

"Not now, Rory," Mrs. Griffen said. "I just heard a car pull in. That must be the Gardners, here to pick up Ashleigh."

Rory peeked out the window. "Yup," he said just as Caroline shouted up the stairwell that Mona was here.

"Besides." Ashleigh tapped the big red cowboy hat that her little brother was wearing. "Your cowboy outfit looks really great on you. I'm sure you'll get lots of candy tonight." She turned Rory around and pointed him toward the door. "Just be sure you save some for me."

They padded down the stairs. Mona was waiting in the living room.

"Wow! Your Cossack horseman costume turned out great!" Ashleigh said as she took in the brightly colored materials and the fancy hat that perched on Mona's head. Mona had worn her high black English riding boots to put the finishing touch on the outfit.

"We'll make a great team," Mona said as she fussed over Ashleigh's red jockey silks and white jockey pants. "You've even got the real boots!" Mona cried.

Ashleigh shifted from foot to foot. "They were a little big, so my mom had to put newspaper in the toes. But I'll grow into them in a couple of years. Rhoda said she'd be honored if I wore them in my first race."

There was a moment of silence when Ashleigh and Mona just stared at each other. The big question of whether Mona would ever get to see Ashleigh race hung in the air between them.

A car horn sounded, breaking the awkward moment. "Let's go to the party!" Ashleigh said, deciding that she was going to have a good time with Mona there.

True to their word, Jamie and Lynne had outdone themselves on the decorations. There were carved pumpkins and cutout black crepe paper cats, white-sheeted ghosts, and bowls full of candy. Jamie's dad called the race for the Halloween Triple Crown, and Ashleigh won the first two races. She was beat out by Mona in the final race.

Ashleigh smiled as she looked around the party at everyone having a good time. It felt great to have fun again. It had been so long since she had really laughed and enjoyed herself. Her only concern was that Mona seemed to be in a down mood this evening.

Ashleigh did everything she could to try to cheer her up, even promising to go riding with her the next day, but she still couldn't snap her friend out of her melancholy.

Later that night, when the Gardners dropped her off and Mona helped Ashleigh lug her party prizes to the door, Ashleigh found the reason for her friend's sadness.

"What's the matter?" Ashleigh asked as she took the

bag of candy from Mona and set it on the porch. "I'm the one who's been in such a bad mood lately. What happened?"

Mona sniffed and wiped at a tear that spilled onto her cheek. "Somebody made an offer on our house, Ash. My parents accepted the offer. . . ."

9

Ashleigh felt like someone had just knocked the air out of her. "No!" she cried as she threw her arms around Mona, hugging her like she would never let her go. "You can't leave. We're best friends! Best friends don't leave!" Ashleigh breathed deep, trying to hold back the tears. She had cried so often these last several weeks, it was starting to feel like a daily routine. "When do you leave?" Ashleigh closed her eyes, not sure if she really wanted to hear the answer.

"We're not sure yet," Mona answered.

Ashleigh released Mona and sat down heavily on the steps, looking up at her friend through the light of the moon. "There's always a lot of paperwork," she said hopefully. "Sometimes these things take months. We might even get to spend Thanksgiving *and* Christmas together."

Mona plopped down on the steps beside Ashleigh.

She plucked at the peeling paint on the porch railing. "I wish," she said wistfully. "But my mom says these people were already approved for a loan. The paperwork should go fast. We might be gone before Thanksgiving."

Ashleigh sat in silence. Although Mona was sitting right next to her and Ashleigh's family was in the house, she had never felt so alone in her life as she did at that moment. There was an empty ache inside her that kept growing and growing until she felt like she was going to choke. She bolted to her feet and stumbled into the house, leaving Mona sitting by herself on the porch.

"Whoa, Ash, what's the matter?" Caroline called out in surprise as Ashleigh streaked up the stairs, taking them two at a time.

Ashleigh ignored her sister and continued on until she reached her bedroom. She didn't bother getting into her pajamas. She pulled off her boots and climbed into bed, pulling the covers over her head for protection like she had when she was Rory's age. But she knew it was no good. Nothing could protect her from the horrible truth of losing her best friend.

"Ashleigh?" Caroline called as she walked softly into the room.

Ashleigh felt the mattress sag as Caroline sat down on the bed.

"Ashleigh, don't cry," Caroline said as she pulled back the covers and stroked Ashleigh's hair. "What's wrong? Is it Mona? Did they sell their house?"

Ashleigh only managed a nod between sobs. She cried so hard, it became difficult to breathe. Caroline stayed on the edge of the bed, patting her shoulder and offering her tissues. There were times when Ashleigh didn't like her sister very much, but at this moment she was glad they were sisters.

"How about if tomorrow I take you shopping?" Caroline suggested. "I've got a lot of money saved up from my allowance. I'll buy you something nice, okay?"

Ashleigh nodded. She still didn't trust herself to speak.

Caroline handed Ashleigh her pajamas. "Here, why don't you get out of your costume? You'll sleep better in these."

Ashleigh sat up, feeling sluggish and groggy. She took off her jockey clothes and piled them next to her bed, then slipped on her pajamas and got back under the covers. She stared at the ceiling. She had no more tears left to cry.

When morning came, she wasn't even sure she had slept. Her entire night was spent thinking of all the fun things Mona and she had done and all the good things they'd miss out on when Mona left for California.

Mrs. Griffen poked her head into the bedroom. "Are you ready to get up, Ashleigh? I've made your favorite breakfast—waffles with strawberries and whipped cream." She paused a moment. "When we're done with breakfast, I'm going to take you and Caroline into the big mall in Lexington. You can skip your chores today."

Ashleigh managed a smile for her mother. "Thanks, Mom. I'll be right down." She didn't feel much like eating, but she knew her mother had worked hard to prepare her favorite breakfast. She slipped on her good jeans and a long-sleeved shirt, then hesitated with her hand over her boots. She eyed her white tennis shoes, then picked them up and put them on her feet. She went down to breakfast.

"Good morning, Ashleigh," Rory chirped as he crammed a large strawberry into his mouth. The whipped cream smeared over half of his face, and the syrup landed on his shirtfront. "I'm going to stay home with Dad today and do your stalls so you can go to the mall with Mom and Caroline and forget about Mona moving away."

Ashleigh saw her mother cut Rory a warning look. "It's okay, Mom. He means well." Ashleigh picked up her fork and stabbed the waffle. She managed to down a couple of bites. It was nice to know her family cared enough to try to make her feel better.

Mrs. Griffen changed the subject, steering the conversation toward plans for the upcoming holidays. "Maybe we could start our Christmas shopping today?" she suggested.

Ashleigh knew her mother was trying to make her feel better, but thinking about the holidays without Mona only made her feel worse. They finished their breakfast and got ready to leave for the mall.

"Do you want to swing by the barn and say good morning to Stardust?" Caroline asked.

Ashleigh eyed the barn and felt her heart begin to ache. Looking at Stardust would only remind her of riding with Mona and Frisky. She shook her head and opened the car door, climbing inside and settling in the backseat. She tried to ignore the big Sold sign that stood on Mona's lawn as they drove past.

The rest of the day passed in a blur. Ashleigh felt so out of it that she actually let her sister talk her into trying on clothes and looking at nail polish. Caroline bought Ashleigh a skirt-and-sweater combination and offered to take her to the school dance after the football game on Saturday night so she could show them off.

They met up with several of Caroline's friends at the mall. Ashleigh was surprised that they weren't as bad as she'd thought. All they wanted to talk about was boys, movie stars, and clothing styles, but they were nice to her, so Ashleigh didn't mind much. It was easy to get pulled along with the crowd when you didn't care much about anything else.

The following week passed in a haze. Ashleigh found herself avoiding Mona whenever she could. It hurt too much to be with her and know these were their last days together. She wanted to cry every time she looked at her friend.

Ashleigh felt the same way about the barn. She did her share of the chores, but she didn't feel much like riding, and she didn't want to go anywhere near the weanlings.

On Saturday, Mona rode over on Frisky and invited Ashleigh to go for a ride.

"It's a beautiful day," Mona said as she tucked her scarf around her neck. "A little cold, maybe." She laughed. "But the sun is shining."

Ashleigh leaned on the pitchfork she was holding and scuffed the toe of her boot in the dirt. "I can't," she said without looking up at Mona. "I promised Caroline I'd go to the game with her. She wants me to go to the dance afterward."

"I could go to the football game," Mona said. "I'll just take Frisky for a short ride. I can be back in time to change and be ready to go."

Ashleigh hung her head. "We're going with Caroline's friends. I don't think they have any room," she mumbled. Mona was so silent, Ashleigh had to look up to see what was happening. She wished she hadn't. The look on Mona's face was terrible. She looked shocked and sad. Ashleigh could see the tears pooling in her eyes.

Mona wheeled Frisky around and heeled her into a canter.

"Mona, wait!" Ashleigh cried as she threw down the pitchfork and ran across the grass. "Maybe I could ask . . . "

But Mona kept riding. Ashleigh watched until she disappeared from sight, then turned and walked slowly back to the barn. She felt worse than ever now.

"What was that all about?" Mrs. Griffen asked as she exited the barn, pushing her loaded wheelbarrow toward the manure pile.

Ashleigh picked up her discarded pitchfork. "Mona wanted me to go for a ride. I told her I couldn't go."

Mrs. Griffen set down the wheelbarrow and studied Ashleigh. "Honey, are you sure you wouldn't much rather go for a ride with Mona than go to the game with Caroline and her friends? I'm sure your sister would understand if you stayed home."

"No, I told Caroline I'd go with her." Ashleigh stared off in the direction of Mona's house. "I can go riding another time." She frowned. At this point she wasn't sure if Mona would even want to go riding with her.

"You know, Ash," Mrs. Griffen said as she settled her earmuffs more firmly on her head. "You can't run away from your problems. You don't have much time left to spend with Mona. You should treasure the moments you have."

Ashleigh stood there, contemplating her mother's words. She knew her mom was right, but it just hurt too much to spend time with Mona.

"Your father and I are going to the auction after we've dropped you girls off at the game," Mrs. Griffen said. "We've made arrangements with the other parents to bring you home."

"Dad said you might buy another mare." Ashleigh leaned on the cleaning fork, waiting for an answer.

Mrs. Griffen nodded. "There are several good mares we're looking at."

"I don't understand it!" Ashleigh exploded. "You got rid of the best horse on the farm! Why would you sell Shadow and then buy another horse? Shadow was the best. We could have kept her for a broodmare!" Ashleigh felt the tears spring to her eyes. She knew she shouldn't talk to her parents like this, but she couldn't understand how they could make a decision like that. They didn't need another broodmare.

"Ashleigh." Mrs. Griffen sighed. "You know we need to keep our stock diversified. And it will be years before Shadow is old enough to breed. We found her a good home with a trainer who can take her to the top. What more could you want?"

Ashleigh balled her fist. The tears clouded her eyes, so she couldn't even see her mother's face. She wasn't sure what she wanted at the moment. She just knew that *nothing* was working out right. Shadow was gone, and soon Mona would be, too. It was too much to bear. Ashleigh turned and ran to the house.

An hour later she came down the stairs and apologized to her family. Her mother gave her another lecture on facing her problems, but Ashleigh felt she was getting off easy—considering the tantrum she had thrown.

She readied herself for the day out with Caroline, feeling funny in her new skirt and sweater. She felt even more strange as the day wore on and she realized that she really didn't fit in with Caroline's friends. They were older than she was, and just like at the mall, the only things they liked talking about were boys, movie stars, and clothes.

Luckily Ashleigh spotted Jamie and Lynne in the crowd and was able to hang around with them for the rest of the game. Jamie's dad gave Ashleigh a ride home afterward, so she didn't have to go to the dance.

Ashleigh thanked Jamie's father for the ride home, then went to the house to change into her jeans. She smiled as she pulled on her boots. They felt much more comfortable than the fancy shoes she had worn. She looked out her bedroom window, staring guiltily toward the barn. Maybe she should go down and pay a visit to Stardust. She'd been neglecting her something horrible lately.

Ashleigh made her way out to the barn. It was quiet except for the faint strains of music coming from Jonas's old radio. Her parents and Rory were at the sale. Jonas was probably taking an afternoon nap. She went to the tack room and grabbed a handful of carrots.

Stardust whinnied and trotted up to the fence when Ashleigh approached. The chestnut mare gobbled up the carrots, then hung her head over the fence, nuzzling Ashleigh for attention.

"Sorry I haven't been around much, girl," Ashleigh apologized. She ran her hands over Stardust's furry winter coat, scratching her on the neck and behind the ears. "The weather's getting awfully cold, but maybe we can go for a ride later."

Ashleigh cocked her head at the sound of a vehicle coming down the driveway. There was no mistaking the sound of the horse trailer bumping over the gravel road. She left Stardust and ran to the front of the barn just as her parents pulled to a halt in front of the stable.

Ashleigh could hear the sounds of a horse moving within the trailer. Curiosity got the better of her, and she came closer to see what her parents had bought at the sale. She waited while her mother opened the manger door to untie the horse within while her father opened the back of the trailer.

Rory hopped down from the old pickup and ran to Ashleigh. "Wait till you see what we bought!" he said excitedly. "I wanted her to be *my* horse, but Mom and Dad say she's going to be your responsi . . ." Rory contorted the word, then tried again. "Responsibility," he continued, proud that he could say the big word.

Ashleigh watched as the mystery horse backed slowly from the trailer. She gasped as she recognized the little gray mare with the swollen belly. Her parents had bought old Pop Potter's sorriest mare!

10

Ashleigh stared in disbelief. Of all the broodmares at the sale, her parents had picked the worst one. She exhaled a long, disappointed sigh. This was what her parents considered a good replacement for Shadow? Not only was the mare terribly underweight; it looked like she was due to foal within the month. Everyone knew that registered horses all celebrated their birthday on January 1. If the foal was born in November, it would be considered a year old on New Year's Day. That would be a big disadvantage during its early race years.

"Remember this little gal, Ashleigh?" Mr. Griffen said.

Ashleigh was speechless. Her parents had to be losing their minds. This was no Edgardale broodmare.

"We got her for a good price," Mr. Griffen continued. "She doesn't look like much now. But with the proper care and feeding, she'll be as good as new. Come hold her while your mother and I take off her leg wraps." He handed the lead rope to Ashleigh.

The little mare stepped forward, touched her muzzle to Ashleigh's shoulder, and nickered.

"See, she likes you already." Mrs. Griffen smiled.

Ashleigh felt a flicker of delight, but she immediately squashed it. She was *not* going to fall in love with this scrawny mare—and especially not her foal! From the looks of the mare, the foal would probably be lucky to survive.

"Why would you buy a horse like this?" Ashleigh cried. "She looks awful! She's nothing like an Edgardale mare."

"Ashleigh," Mrs. Griffen said in a voice that warned she was losing her patience. "You don't know anything about this mare."

Ashleigh scrunched her lips and stared at the little bay. "I know she's skinny, and she's due way too late in the season, and she's *no* replacement for Shadow!"

Mrs. Griffen tossed the leg wraps into the tack compartment of the trailer. "That'll be enough, Ashleigh," she warned. "Your father and I have let a lot of things slide because we know you're going through a rough time right now. But that doesn't give you the right to behave badly. This mare is going to be your responsibility. Her name is Special Prize, and I expect you to treat her just like all the other broodmares on this property." She looked Ashleigh in the eye. "Do I make myself clear?"

Ashleigh nodded. Her parents could force her to care for the mare, but they couldn't make her love the little gray.

Mr. Griffen took the mare's lead rope and handed Ashleigh some papers. "I'll put Prize away while you go file her papers in the office."

Ashleigh carried the Jockey Club registration and several other papers to the barn office. She closed the door so her parents couldn't hear her grumbling. She jerked open the file drawer and looked for the folder that held the registration papers.

Ashleigh's eyes caught several of the words that stood out on the top paper. *Accidental breeding* and *possibly due in late November* were among the comments. She found the folder she was looking for and tossed the papers inside. But curiosity got the better of her. She retrieved the papers and scanned them quickly before her parents came.

Just as she suspected, the mare was due soon. A veterinary inspection was attached to Prize's papers, saying that the mare had been examined and it was determined that she might have trouble foaling.

There was nothing here that Ashleigh hadn't already guessed. She hesitated when she came to the

Jockey Club papers, her eyes lingering on the mare's pedigree.

Ashleigh gasped in surprise. Prize was sired by Northern Dancer, a horse considered by most to have been the top sire in the country until his death a few years ago. She couldn't believe her eyes. She turned the papers over in her hands, searching to see if they were fake, but she'd studied too many pedigrees not to know the real thing when she saw it. She heard footfalls outside the office door and quickly dropped the file back into the cabinet.

A moment later Mr. Griffen entered the office. "Grab one of those feed charts, would you, Ash? I want to get Prize set up on a feeding program. We're going to have to watch her very carefully for a while. Her condition is bad—she might colic if she gets too much food or something that's too rich for her."

Ashleigh fetched one of the feeding charts for her father. She wrote Prize's name at the top.

"Let's keep her on straight grass hay for a couple of days," Mr. Griffen said. "No grain and no alfalfa."

Ashleigh looked up from her notes. "But she needs to put on some weight. Wouldn't some grain and alfalfa help?"

Mr. Griffen patted Ashleigh's shoulder. "Eventually we'll work that hotter feed into her diet, but right now I'm concerned that it would upset her digestive system and cause a colic. As close as Prize is to foaling, it might make her lose the foal."

Ashleigh frowned. As small as Edgardale's breeding operation was, they couldn't afford to lose a single foal. Especially a foal whose grandsire was Northern Dancer. But would the foal be able to race? Ashleigh wondered. The papers had said *accidental breeding.* Maybe the sire wasn't even a Thoroughbred. "Who was the stallion Prize was bred to?" Ashleigh asked.

Mr. Griffen smiled. "That's part of the reason I bought this mare." He pulled a photocopied set of papers from his inside pocket. "Remember that nice racing stallion Potter's neighbor had for a while? The one who won the Breeders' Cup two years ago?"

Ashleigh furrowed her brow as she took the copies from her father. "Yes, but that colt hasn't been put out to stud yet," she said. "They haven't bred any mares to him."

"Not on purpose." Mr. Griffen laughed.

Ashleigh's eyes grew wide. "Prize's foal is sired by Storm Catcher?"

Mr. Griffen nodded. "They're not planning on retiring Storm Catcher to stud until next season. He jumped the fence and got in with Prize. And we've got the only foal of his."

Ashleigh sat back in her chair. She was impressed. Her parents had made a better deal than she originally thought. But still, she had no intention of getting close to any more of the foals. She would care for Prize, but she would not get attached to the mare or her foal. She picked up her pencil, waiting for the rest of her father's directions.

"Let's give her a little hot bran mash," Mr. Griffen instructed. "But no grain yet. Let's make sure she can handle the bland food before we throw the high-protein rations to her." He looked directly at Ashleigh. "This is going to be a big responsibility, Ashleigh. Your mother and I trust you to handle it."

Ashleigh nodded. "I won't let you down, Dad."

"I know you won't." Mr. Griffen ruffled her hair. "That's why I'm giving the job to you."

"Ashleigh?" Mrs. Griffen's voice sounded from outside the office door. "Mona is here to see you."

Ashleigh felt her stomach drop. So far, this day had pretty much been a disaster. She really didn't want to see Mona right now. What if Mona was here to tell her that she was leaving tomorrow? She sat where she was, chewing on the pencil eraser and staring at Prize's chart.

"Well?" Mr. Griffen said. "Are you going to keep Mona waiting?"

Ashleigh put down the pencil and walked out of the office to meet her friend. Mona smiled, and Ashleigh attempted to smile back, but she was sure it wasn't a very good smile. It felt kind of sickly on her face. Ashleigh felt so guilty for not spending time with Mona, but every time they were together, all they talked about were the plans and dreams they had made together that would never get to be now that Mona was moving to the other side of the United States.

"I saw the horse trailer and came to see what your parents brought home," Mona said. "Did they get another broodmare?"

Ashleigh nodded. "She's in Shadow's old stall." They stood there for several awkward moments. Ashleigh crammed her hands into her jean pockets. She hated feeling like this. She and Mona were best friends. She wasn't supposed to feel uncomfortable around her—but she did. Part of it was guilt for not spending as much time around her friend as she should, and part of it was not wanting to feel the big hurt that Ashleigh knew would come on Mona's final day before she moved.

"Can I see her?" Mona asked hopefully.

Ashleigh nodded and led the way down the aisle. She opened Prize's door and let Mona inside.

"Ashleigh, you didn't tell me you guys bought one of Potter's mares!" Mona exclaimed. "Oh, my gosh! She's so skinny. The poor thing." Mona patted the mare, running her hands across her furry coat and fussing over Prize. The mare stretched her neck and bobbed her head to show Mona she was scratching the right place. "She's going to take a lot of work," Mona said. "But she's really a pretty mare. Prize will look great when she's all fixed up."

"My parents put me in charge of her." Ashleigh leaned against the stall wall. She wanted to pet the mare, too, but she wouldn't let herself. She'd feed Prize and groom her when she had to, but she didn't want to do anything special that might make her change her mind about falling in love with the little gray mare.

Mrs. Griffen hollered from the office doorway, "We're going up to the house, Ashleigh. Bring Mona up for a cup of hot chocolate when you girls are through here."

Mona looked at Ashleigh, waiting for the invitation. When Ashleigh didn't speak right away, Mona's face fell. She quickly turned back to the mare to hide her disappointment. Prize nuzzled her cheek. "Oh, Ashleigh, you're so lucky to have all of these horses."

Ashleigh picked up a long piece of straw and began shredding it. "Yeah, real lucky," she said. "They just end up being sold."

Mona turned at the bitter note in Ashleigh's voice. "You really *are* lucky, Ash. Edgardale raises some great racehorses. We've had a lot of fun with all the babies." She looked wistfully down the barn aisle at all the other broodmares. "I'm really going to miss this place."

Ashleigh felt the comment slice through her, cutting her to the quick. She didn't want to hear about Mona leaving! She didn't want to talk about Edgardale babies. She just wanted to go back to her room and forget that she was losing her best friend.

"I need to ask you a favor," Mona said.

Ashleigh nodded.

"When we leave, we won't be able to take Frisky right away," Mona explained. "I was hoping you could keep her and ride her until we get a place for her."

Ashleigh kicked at the straw on the stall floor. She didn't want to look at Mona. Her stomach felt all tied in knots, and the burning in her eyes told her that she was just about to cry again. She could feel Mona's eyes on her as her friend waited for a reply. "Sure," Ashleigh mumbled.

"Great!" Mona said. She gave Prize a final pat and walked out of the stall. "Want to go get that hot chocolate?" She looked around nervously while she waited for Ashleigh's reply. "The weather's getting really cold now."

Ashleigh closed Prize's door, leaning on the cool wood as she stared at the mare, trying to avoid Mona's gaze. "I don't really feel like it."

"Oh," Mona said.

Ashleigh could hear the disappointment in her friend's voice. She knew Mona really wanted to go up to the house, but Ashleigh was sure she wouldn't be able to drink the cocoa without choking on it. It was better that they didn't even try. She pushed away from Prize's door and started down the aisle toward the tack room. She wasn't sure what she was going to do when she got there, but she just didn't feel like talking to Mona about the move.

"How about a ride tomorrow morning?" Mona suggested.

Ashleigh shook her head. "I can't. I've got to take care of Prize. She's going to take a lot of work."

"Then how about after school on Monday?" Mona followed Ashleigh to the tack room.

"No, that won't work, either," Ashleigh said. "I've got a lot of homework on Mondays."

Mona stopped in the middle of the aisle, her hands on her hips. "Well, how about Tuesday?" she said, her voice getting louder and more annoyed. "Or Wednesday? Or are you going to be busy every day until I'm gone?"

Ashleigh whirled around. "It's not like that!" she shouted. "I'm just *busy*, that's all."

"Yeah, busy feeling sorry for yourself," Mona accused.

Ashleigh pursed her lips in a frown. "You don't

understand, Mona. That's not how it is."

Mona crossed her arms and glared at Ashleigh. "Then how is it, Ash? You've got all these great horses, yet you don't want to play with any of them because you're afraid you'll get attached to them and get hurt. I'm *supposed* to be your best friend, but you never want to see me anymore."

Ashleigh glared back at Mona. "You just don't understand."

Mona threw her hands up in exasperation. "You're being so selfish, Ashleigh! Do you think you're the only one hurting? I'm losing my best friend, too! All I want to do is enjoy the time we have left, but you don't even act like you like me anymore."

A sob tore from Mona's throat, and she turned and ran from the barn.

"Mona, wait!" Ashleigh called as she ran after her, but Mona kept running down the driveway, her short brown hair flying in the wind. Ashleigh stopped at Edgardale's gate, her breath wheezing in and out of her lungs. She watched as Mona rounded the corner and turned toward her own house. Ashleigh wondered if she had lost her best friend forever.

11

"Look, Ash," Rory called when Ashleigh entered the house. "I made a paper turkey for our Thanksgiving party." He proudly displayed the multicolored, lopsided bird.

Ashleigh smiled for her little brother's benefit, but inside she was hurting so bad, it was difficult to breathe. She closed the door and went up the stairs to her room. Caroline was at a friend's house. Right now Ashleigh really needed the peace and quiet to think.

Mona was right. Ashleigh *was* being selfish and thinking only of herself. Her parents had been trying to tell her the same thing. But she had been in so much pain, she didn't want to listen. Ashleigh picked up the photo of her and Mona and hugged it to her chest. A tear slid down her cheek. She had really blown it. But how was she going to make things right?

Ashleigh put down the picture and stared out the

window at Mona's house. She was surprised to see Mona leading Frisky from the barn. And the mare was saddled. Mona was going for a ride without her!

Ashleigh reached for her riding boots. She would ride out and follow Mona, then apologize for the entire ride if that's what it took to get Mona to forgive her.

Ashleigh ran down the stairs, her boots hitting every other step as she hurried to catch Mona.

"Ashleigh, where are you going?" Mrs. Griffen called. "Supper is almost ready."

"I'm going riding with Mona," Ashleigh said as she reached for her riding jacket next to the door.

Mrs. Griffen stepped into the living room, a bowl of salad still in her hands. "It's too late for a ride, Ash. Wait and go tomorrow."

Mr. Griffen looked up from the *Racing Form* he was studying on the couch. Ashleigh stared at him, begging him with her eyes to help.

"Let her go, Elaine," Mr. Griffen said. "I think this is important."

"Thanks, Dad," Ashleigh yelled as she slipped on her coat and ran out the door. The breeze was cold. Ashleigh pulled on her riding gloves as she made her way to the barn. The horses were in their stalls, eating hay. Stardust looked surprised to see her. "Sorry, girl," Ashleigh said as she slipped the halter over the mare's head and led her out to the crossties. "We've got to do something."

Ashleigh had Stardust saddled and was out the barn door in less than five minutes. She pointed the chestnut mare down the trail and asked her for a canter. She wanted to catch Mona as quickly as possible.

Stardust felt the heels in her sides and the wind in her tail and snorted. She took several strides, then put down her head and crow-hopped for several more.

"Stardust!" Ashleigh cried in surprise as she tugged at the reins, trying to raise the mare's head. Stardust gave one good buck that almost sent Ashleigh flying over the saddle. "Whoa!" she called as her heart thudded in her chest. Stardust slid to a halt, her tail over her back and her nostrils distended.

Ashleigh took the reins in her shaking left hand as she reached down to pat the mare. "I guess I deserved that," she said. "I haven't been paying much attention lately to you, either." She walked a couple of circles to get Stardust settled down, then asked the mare for a trot until some of her energy was gone. She caught Mona at the gateway to the back field.

"Mona, wait!" Ashleigh called. She saw her friend look back over her shoulder, then heel Frisky into a run in the opposite direction. "Mona!" Ashleigh shouted again, then gave Stardust her head and asked her to run.

Stardust surged ahead, seeming to know how important it was that they catch up to Mona and Frisky. Ashleigh lay low over her withers, asking the mare for everything she had. The cold wind whipped Ashleigh's cheeks as they raced headlong, trying to catch the other racing horse and rider.

They left the immediate field and passed into the next. Ashleigh noted that they were staying about the same distance apart. Stardust was running as fast as she could, but Frisky was pure Thoroughbred. Their only hope of catching up was if Frisky wore herself out and Stardust still had some energy left. "Please, Mona, slow down," Ashleigh whispered under her breath.

In the next moment Ashleigh saw Frisky shy to the right, and Mona floundered in the saddle. Ashleigh could see that Mona had lost her stirrup and was hanging on to Frisky's neck. "Mona!" she cried, hoping that her friend could hang on.

Ashleigh sat up in her own saddle, watching the mishap unfold before her but knowing that there was nothing she could do about it. She held her breath as Mona struggled to stay on Frisky and get the mare stopped. Frisky finally hit the brakes, skidding to a halt with several jolting steps. Mona flew over the mare's shoulder, landing on her feet, then falling to the ground at the impact.

Ashleigh reached her friend, jumping out of the

saddle before Stardust even came to a full stop. "Are you okay?" She knelt beside Mona, looking to see if she had broken anything. She was shocked when Mona started to laugh. Ashleigh rocked back on her heels. "What's so funny?" she asked in dismay.

"Us." Mona laughed even harder. "We both tried running away from our problems, but it didn't work for either of us."

Ashleigh looked at the dirt smudged on Mona's face and started to giggle. "I guess you're right." She helped her friend to her feet. "I'm just glad I didn't have to fall off a horse to figure it out."

They stood in the middle of the road, dusting the dirt of off Mona's pants, and laughed until tears were streaming down their faces. Then Ashleigh sobered. "I *really* am sorry, Mona. I've been such an idiot. I was just hurting so bad, I didn't know how to handle my feelings. I'm sorry I hurt yours."

Mona smiled. "Well, at least you realized what a lunk-head you've been while we still have some time left."

Ashleigh laughed as she helped Mona back on Frisky. "Let's go back to my house for that hot chocolate my mom promised us. We can help Rory cut out some more lopsided turkeys for Thanksgiving."

"Deal!" Mona said. "But how about if we just walk back to the barn?"

They laughed all the way back to Edgardale.

The next week passed quickly. Ashleigh's household was in an uproar as everyone readied the place for the Thanksgiving feast. Ashleigh felt sad every time she saw all the festive decorations and knew that Mona would be gone before the holidays. She was glad that she and Mona were spending more time together. It still hurt, but at least now she had learned to treasure each moment she had left.

Ashleigh still shied away from the weanlings. She fed them and helped her parents and Jonas move them indoors each night now that the weather was turning snowy. But she tried not to get too involved with any of them.

Prize was harder to ignore. The mare had a sweet temperament, and she loved people. She nickered to Ashleigh every time she entered the barn, and she nuzzled her jacket for the carrots that Ashleigh had stored for Stardust. The mare had picked up a few pounds, but she still wasn't allowed a ration of grain like the rest of the horses. Now that the weather was turning really cold, the horses needed the extra energy the grain would provide to help keep them warm.

Ashleigh felt bad for Prize. Each night at feeding time, the little gray mare would stick her head over the stall door and whinny, watching as each bucket of grain was given to the rest of the mares. When her bucket of plain bran mash was delivered to her stall, she ate it gratefully, but Ashleigh knew the mare sensed she was missing something.

"Maybe next week," Derek Griffen had said when Ashleigh asked if she could start adding grain to Prize's mash. "I'm still not one hundred percent happy with her progress. I think she needs a few more days before we start her on some richer feed."

Ashleigh nodded, but she slipped a handful of sweet feed into her jacket pocket to give to Prize at the night feeding.

The vet came to check on Prize at the end of the week. He was still concerned that she might have trouble foaling.

"She's looking a lot better, Derek," Dr. Frankel said as he inspected Prize. "But she's still got a long way to go."

"We're thinking of putting her on a little grain to speed up her weight gain," Mr. Griffen said.

Dr. Frankel looked up from his inspection of the mare. "Why don't you give it one more week, Derek? She's making good progress, but I'm concerned about her foal. Let's not do anything to upset the balance right now."

The vet gave them the name of a good vitamin to start Prize on, then set an appointment for the following week and left.

That night at feeding time Ashleigh helped Jonas with the grain buckets while Rory filled water tanks, and the rest of the family fed the hay. Ashleigh was so deep in thought about the plans for the holidays that she didn't notice she had mixed up the grain buckets until she saw Stardust turn up her nose.

"What's the matter, girl?" Ashleigh said as she dug into the bucket, noticing that there wasn't any grain mixed in with the bran. Ashleigh's pulse quickened. If Stardust had the bran, that meant that Prize was eating the mash with the grain in it!

Ashleigh quickly exited the stall and went to Prize. The little mare was happily munching away at her dinner. Ashleigh entered the stall and pushed Prize's nose out of the bucket. Her heart sank. There was only a handful of grain left. Prize had eaten it all.

Ashleigh sighed. What was she going to do? She didn't want to admit to her parents that she had been daydreaming and messed up.

Prize finished her grain, then came to Ashleigh, lipping her coat as she stared at her with kind brown eyes. "Did it taste good?" Ashleigh asked as she reached out to fondle the mare's muzzle, then quickly withdrew her hand. Ashleigh decided against saying anything to her parents. The ration of grain that Prize had eaten was very small, anyway. Stardust didn't get as much as the broodmares did. Most likely the mare would be fine.

But later that night Ashleigh had to take back that thought. When she entered the barn to say good night to Stardust, Prize was down in her stall, a layer of sweat covering her body as she groaned and nipped at her flanks.

12

Ashleigh pulled open the stall door and dropped to her knees in the straw beside the distressed mare. Prize looked at her through pain-filled eyes, then lay back in the bedding with a groan and attempted to roll. "No, don't roll!" Ashleigh cried.

What was she going to do? This was all her fault! If she hadn't have been daydreaming, she wouldn't have fed the wrong ration to Prize. Ashleigh cocked her head, hearing the lazy sound of music drifting from the upstairs apartment. She scrambled to her feet and ran out of the stall. "Jonas!" she screamed up the old wooden staircase. "Jonas, help!"

At the sound of slippered feet pounding across the upstairs floor, Ashleigh dashed back to check on Prize. The mare now lay out flat on her side, her rounded belly looking grossly distended compared to the rest of her malnourished body.

"What's the problem?" Jonas said as he hurried down the barn aisle, his bathrobe billowing in his wake.

"Prize colicked!" Ashleigh cried. "It's all my fault. I accidentally mixed up the grain buckets. She got Stardust's ration."

Jonas knelt in the straw, placing a comforting hand on the mare's neck. He turned to Ashleigh. "Go get your parents, and tell them to call the vet. I'm going to get this mare up and get her walking."

Ashleigh bolted out of the barn and ran as fast as she could to the house. "Prize is colicking!" she cried as she burst through the door. "Jonas says to call the vet."

Ashleigh followed her parents back to the barn. Jonas had Prize up and walking, but the mare was in obvious distress.

"What happened?" Mr. Griffen asked as he took over the walking from Jonas.

The old groom scratched his head. "She seemed fine when I did my final check an hour ago. Ashleigh says she accidentally got a ration of grain tonight." He looked apologetically at Ashleigh.

Ashleigh hung her head. "It's all my fault," she said. "Prize is sick because I fed her grain."

Mr. Griffen's brows rose. "You gave Prize grain after I specifically told you she couldn't have any?"

Ashleigh felt miserable. She looked at Prize as the mare labored up and down the barn aisle, her head drooped so low, it almost touched the ground. "I didn't do it on purpose," she said. "I wasn't paying attention, and I gave her Stardust's bucket."

Mr. Griffen breathed a sigh of relief. "Well, at least it wasn't one of the other broodmares' rations."

"I'm so sorry!" Ashleigh started to cry.

Mrs. Griffen put her arm around Ashleigh's shoulders. "It's okay, Ashleigh. We all make mistakes. You didn't do it on purpose."

"But she could die!" Ashleigh cried. "And it will be all my fault!"

"Well, there's no doubt that the mistake might have been avoided if you'd been paying closer attention," Mr. Griffen agreed. "But we're not sure that the mix-up is what caused this colic. We don't give Stardust that much grain."

The sound of the vet's truck pulling up to the barn caught everyone's attention.

"Good, he's here," Mrs. Griffen said as she went to greet the vet.

Dr. Frankel checked the sick mare, going over every detail and asking questions. After a few minutes he looked up and smiled. "The good news is, she doesn't have a twisted gut."

Everyone sighed in relief.

"But she is one sick little mare," the vet said as he put away his stethoscope and prepared a shot of bute. "Walk her for a couple more minutes, then put her back in her stall." He handed the lead rope to Ashleigh.

Ashleigh tried to catch fragments of the conversation as she passed back and forth down the aisle. Dr. Frankel thought Prize would survive the colic, but he was worried that it might set off an early delivery.

"Go ahead and put her back in her stall," the vet instructed. He handed some extra bute to Mr. Griffen. "Call me if you have any more trouble."

Ashleigh led Prize back into her stall. Maybe it was the extra handfuls of grain that Ashleigh had been sneaking the mare in her pocket that had caused this trouble. Ashleigh frowned. If she hadn't started feeling sorry for the little mare, this probably wouldn't have happened. She took off Prize's halter and reminded herself of her promise not to fall in love with any more of the horses.

Prize's health improved over the following days. With the preparations for the coming holiday and the rush to get schoolwork finished before the break, Ashleigh didn't have much time to spend with the horses or Mona.

Every time Ashleigh visited Mona's house, she was busy packing. The sale of their property was moving along, and it looked like they would be leaving for their new home in California the day before Thanksgiving.

Ashleigh paused in her math homework, staring out the window toward Mona's house. A light snow was falling, blowing in spiral patterns across the lawn.

Ashleigh wondered what Mona was doing at this moment. Now that their time was short, it was getting more and more painful to spend time together. Each night when they said good-bye, it was like a piece of Ashleigh's heart chipped away. How was she ever going to be able to look Mona in the eye and say that final good-bye?

A knock on the door pulled Ashleigh from her sad thoughts.

"Ash?" Mr. Griffen rapped softly on the bedroom door, then poked his head into the room. "Looks like tonight might be Prize's night. You want to go on foal watch with me?"

Ashleigh chewed the tip of her pencil. She loved foal watch with her father, but she really didn't want to see the birth of the new foal. What was the point? It would only make her feel more strongly toward the foal, and she had promised herself that she wasn't going to get attached to them anymore. "Um." She hesitated, not wanting to hurt her father's feelings. "I'm kind of tired. I think I'll just sleep in the house tonight." She looked down at her math text, not wanting to see her father's face.

"Come on, Ash," Mr. Griffen said as he walked farther into the room. "I know how you felt about Shadow being sold."

Ashleigh's head snapped up at the mention of Shadow.

Her father continued. "I know you're afraid you'll get hurt again. But we live on a horse farm, Ashleigh. You can't avoid the foals forever."

Ashleigh picked at the edge of her notebook. Her father was right about one thing . . . she couldn't avoid the foals. But she *could* avoid falling in love with them. She looked at her dad's hopeful expression and nodded. "Okay, I'll be down as soon as I'm finished with my homework."

The snow was falling steadily when Ashleigh made her way to the barn. She looked up into the sky, watching the light flakes dance toward the earth. Shadow had been born on a night like this. Only it had been a much worse storm, and it was at the correct time of the year! Ashleigh found herself worrying about the difficulties the little foal would face because he was being born at the wrong time of the year. That was—*if* the foal even lived.

Ashleigh settled into the warm tack room with her father and began the long wait. They played cards and board games until she couldn't keep her eyes open any longer. In the wee hours of the morning, her father woke her to tell her Prize was in labor.

They didn't go into the stall like Ashleigh had when Shadow was born. Instead they waited in the barn aisle, keeping a close watch by the dim light of a distant bulb. Just before sunrise Prize delivered a healthy colt.

Ashleigh felt the tears spring to her eyes. Watching a new life come into this world was always something special. She felt the pull of her heart and quickly turned aside. But she found her eyes wandering back to watch the new colt take his first faltering steps.

"Look at how perfect he is," Mr. Griffen said as he entered the stall to doctor the umbilical cord.

"Who would have thought that skinny a mare would throw a colt so healthy?" Ashleigh agreed.

Mr. Griffen smiled. "That's one of the miracles of nature. These mares give everything they've got to their unborn babies. That's how they ensure the continuation of the species." He poured iodine on the foal's umbilical cord, then turned his attention to Prize. "Prize is looking a little worn out. I'll put a call in to Dr. Frankel at first light."

"Is she going to be okay?" Ashleigh bit her lip as she looked in on the small mare, lying in the straw. "She looks really weak."

"I don't think there were any complications," Mr. Griffen said. "But I don't want to take a chance with Prize as poor as her condition is. I'll stay in the barn and keep an eye on her until Dr. Frankel gets here."

He looked at Ashleigh. "You want to name the colt before you go?"

Ashleigh shook her head vigorously. "It's Rory's turn," she protested. But the truth was, she didn't want to give a special name to a colt that she didn't want to care about.

Mr. Griffen wiped the extra moisture from the foal's coat, moving the little guy around so Prize could help clean him up. "You're looking pretty tired," he said to Ashleigh. "Why don't you go on up to the house? I'll finish up here."

Ashleigh yawned as she trudged through the newly fallen snow toward the house. The sun was just breaking over the horizon. The memory of watching the little brown colt take his first steps made her smile. If she were going to name the colt, she'd call him Morning Prize.

Ashleigh woke around eleven. She stretched and threw back the covers, then peered out the window. The snow had stopped, but there was at least four inches of it on the ground. She gazed toward the barn, surprised to see Dr. Frankel's truck still parked in the driveway.

Ashleigh felt a pricking of dread. The veterinarian should have been gone a long time ago. Something must have gone wrong. She jumped out of bed and pulled on her clothes. Caroline was sitting in the living room with Rory when Ashleigh came downstairs. "Where's Mom and Dad?" She tried to keep her voice even, but she could hear the worry in it.

Caroline had a concerned look on her face. "Prize had a few problems. They're all down at the barn with the vet."

Ashleigh pulled on her coat and ran out to the barn. She tried to tell herself that she didn't care about the little mare, but she picked up her pace just the same. After all, Prize *was* her responsibility.

Dr. Frankel was just leaving as Ashleigh entered the barn. "How is she?" Ashleigh asked.

Dr. Frankel shook his head. "She's a lucky little horse. There was some internal bleeding that your father couldn't see, but we got her fixed up. All we can do now is keep her quiet and see what happens. The rest is up to her."

Ashleigh went to look in on the little gray mare. She was lying in the straw while her foal shuffled around her, nibbling at her mane and tail. Ashleigh felt the tug on her heartstrings again, but she pushed the feeling aside. She *really* didn't want to get involved with the mare now. The way Dr. Frankel was talking, Prize could die.

Mrs. Griffen stood behind Ashleigh and put her hands on her shoulders. "Prize really needs you now, Ash."

Ashleigh took a deep breath. "Could Caroline keep watch on her?"

Mrs. Griffen gently squeezed Ashleigh's shoulders. "We could assign her to Caroline, but we know that you're this mare's best shot. I'll leave it up to you, but Prize needs all the help she can get, Ashleigh."

Ashleigh watched the foal play. After a while he began to poke Prize with his nose, making a smacking noise with his tongue and lips as he tried to get his mother to stand so he could nurse. What would happen to Morning Prize if his mother died? Ashleigh wondered. Would he die, too? She turned to her mother. "I'll do it, Mom."

Mrs. Griffen smiled and hugged Ashleigh. "I was really hoping you would say that. Now I know Prize is in good hands."

Ashleigh spent the next several days coming home from school and spending time on sick watch for Prize and her foal. Sometimes Mona came with her, and they did their homework in the tack room. Other times Ashleigh was alone. On the Monday before Thanksgiving, Mona broke the bad news—the house was closing escrow the following day, and they would be flying to their new home on Wednesday, the day before the holiday.

"I can't believe the time has gone so fast," Mona said.

Ashleigh stood outside Prize and Morning's stall, watching the little colt nurse. Ashleigh had finally suggested to her parents the name Morning Prize for the colt, and they'd agreed it was perfect. Prize had gained some strength over the last few days, but she wasn't out of danger yet. She was still pathetically skinny, and her foal was drinking down all the mare's extra nutrition. "I know, I can't believe it, either," Ashleigh agreed. "Now that the time is really here, I just feel numb inside."

Mona leaned her chin on the stall door and nodded. "I wish we could have at least spent Thanksgiving together."

"Want to come for dinner tonight?" Ashleigh asked. "We're having chicken, but we can pretend it's turkey."

"Sure." Mona nodded. "Let me call my mom and ask."

That night at dinner Ashleigh felt like she was going to choke every time she swallowed. She couldn't help thinking that it would only be a couple more days until Mona was gone.

Later, when Ashleigh said good-bye to Mona on the front porch steps, she got a real dose of what it was going to be like at that final good-bye. As she waved to Mona with tears in her eyes, she wondered how she was ever going to be able to stop herself from shattering into a million pieces.

13

Wednesday arrived in a haze of gray skies and snow flurries. Ashleigh felt just like the weather that played outside her bedroom window—cold and dreary. She lay in bed and cracked the curtain, staring toward Mona's house. She could see Mrs. Gardner loading their things into their car.

Ashleigh sighed and lay back on the mattress, staring at the ceiling. Maybe if she didn't get out of bed, she wouldn't have to start this day, and Mona wouldn't have to leave. She frowned. That kind of stuff only happened in fairy tales.

"Ashleigh." Mrs. Griffen knocked lightly on the door, then poked her head into the room. "Mona's flight leaves in a couple of hours. She'll be here in a little while to say good-bye."

Ashleigh nodded. She looked over at Caroline in

the next bed. Her sister was wide awake and staring back at her.

"Are you going to be all right, Ash?" Caroline said with concern. "I know what a hard time you've been having." She rolled onto her side, facing Ashleigh. "You haven't been yourself lately."

Ashleigh wondered if she would ever be the same again. "Yeah, I'll be okay, Caro," she said, more for her sister's benefit than because she thought it was so. "It's just going to be really different without Mona here. Who am I going to ride with?"

"Maybe Jamie and Lynne," Caroline suggested.

Ashleigh sat up in bed and stretched her legs over the side. She shrugged. "Jamie and Lynne live a couple of miles away. It would take them a long time to get here if I just wanted to go for a quick ride."

Caroline was silent for several moments. Her voice was sincere when she spoke. "Look, Ash, I know you and I don't always see things the same way. But I'm really sorry about Mona moving. If you need anything, I'll be here for you."

Ashleigh managed a smile for her sister. "Thanks, Caro."

Caroline got out of bed and put on her housecoat, then padded down the stairs, leaving Ashleigh to herself.

Ashleigh got slowly out of bed, not wanting to rush

to the moment when she would see Mona for the last time. She picked her socks out of the drawer, mulling over several different colors before choosing the blue ones. She chose her pants and shirt the same way.

Ashleigh heard a knock on the door as she was slipping on her boots. She glanced at the clock. It had to be Mona. She sat on the edge of her bed, feeling trapped. Panic welled inside her. She had been dreading this moment for a long time. She had thought she could be brave, but now that the time was here, Ashleigh didn't know what to do.

"Ashleigh," Mrs. Griffen called from the bottom of the stairs. "Mona's here."

Ashleigh willed herself to get off the bed and move toward the door, but she couldn't. She sat frozen in place, unable to obey her mind's commands.

"Ashleigh?" Mrs. Griffen called.

Ashleigh could hear Mona's voice drifting up the stairwell. A sharp pain raced through her as she realized this would be the last time she would hear Mona's voice in person for a long time—if ever again.

"Ashleigh!" Her father's voice echoed loudly from below.

Ashleigh gathered her courage and forced herself to stand. As much as she dreaded it, she had to say goodbye to her best friend—even if it hurt worse than anything she'd ever done before.

With leaden feet, she moved toward the bedroom door and down the stairs. *Be brave. You can do this without crying,* she told herself. But when she reached the bottom of the stairs and saw Mona standing there with her shoulders slumped and her eyes bright with tears, Ashleigh knew that she couldn't be brave. She knew in that moment that she was the biggest coward on earth.

Ashleigh turned and bolted across the living room. A sob tore from her throat as she ran out the back door. She wasn't sure where she was going. She only knew she had to hide where nobody could find her.

The snow was falling lightly, but Ashleigh didn't care. She didn't feel it. She couldn't feel anything at the moment except the huge, aching void that seemed to take up all of her insides. She spotted the barn and headed for it, bursting through the doors without stopping or looking behind her.

Several of the horses jumped and snorted as Ashleigh raced past their stalls, heading for the ladder that led to the hayloft. She pulled herself up the ladder and stumbled across the bales of hay. When she reached the farthest corner of the loft, she finally quit running and sank to her knees, gasping for breath between sobs and hiccups. She had never been more miserable in her life.

Ashleigh lay in the scratchy, sweet-smelling hay and

cried for herself and Mona. Mona probably thought she was awful for running out on her, but Ashleigh just couldn't have faced her.

Between sniffles and chokes Ashleigh could hear her family moving around the property, calling for her. Somebody even came up the ladder and looked in the loft, but Ashleigh had smashed herself against the hay, and the person hadn't seen her.

After a while the tears wouldn't come anymore, so she just sat there in misery, wondering what Mona was going through at the moment. Ashleigh despised herself for being such a coward. Mona probably felt worse than ever now.

Ashleigh heard the muted sound of someone climbing the steep ladder steps. She held her breath, hoping they would go away, but whoever it was climbed the last rung and stepped into the hayloft.

"Ashleigh?" Mrs. Griffen called softly. "Ashleigh, I know you're in here." She waited for several more moments. "I know you're here because this is where you used to come when you were a little girl and your feelings got hurt."

"I'm over here, Mom." Ashleigh leaned out from behind the bales of hay.

Mrs. Griffen made her way carefully through the hay pile and took a seat next to Ashleigh, pulling her into her arms. "I'm here for you, Ashleigh," she said.

Ashleigh curled into her mother's arms. "Mona must really hate me," she cried. "I don't know why I ran away. I just couldn't stand to say good-bye."

"It's not too late to set things right," Mrs. Griffen said as she set Ashleigh at arm's length and offered her a smile.

Ashleigh gasped. "Is Mona still here?"

Mrs. Griffen shook her head. "No, but her plane doesn't leave for another forty-five minutes. I bet you could catch her on the courtesy phone in the airport."

Ashleigh decided it was time to put away her tears and do what was right. She untangled her legs and stood. If she used the phone here in the barn, she wouldn't waste any time. She stepped carefully down the ladder and went to check on Prize and Morning while her mother looked up the number.

"Here it is," Mrs. Griffen said as she handed the phone to Ashleigh.

Ashleigh's hands shook while she waited for the operator to connect her to Mona. Would Mona even answer the phone? Would she want to talk to Ashleigh? A moment later Mona's choked voice came across the telephone line.

Ashleigh could have jumped for joy. She poured out her heart, telling Mona how sorry she was. "I feel so rotten for running out on you," Ashleigh said. "I'm such a coward!"

Ashleigh breathed a sigh of relief when Mona forgave her for being such an idiot. They talked for another ten minutes, then Mona had to catch her plane. Before they hung up, Mona invited Ashleigh out to spend the summer with her in California. The only thing that could have made Ashleigh happier was if Mona had stayed.

Ashleigh spent the rest of the day hanging around the barn and keeping an eye on Prize and her new foal. Her mother and Caroline were in the house, preparing things for tomorrow's big Thanksgiving Day feast. Since Ashleigh wasn't much help in the kitchen, she decided to spend the day in the barn.

Several times she picked up the phone to call Mona about something, then she remembered that her friend was probably at her new home by now. It felt really weird and sad, not having her best friend around.

Ashleigh picked up the grooming kit, deciding that brushing a few horses might help keep her mind off Mona. But by the time she had gone through most of the barn, she still felt the empty ache of losing her best friend.

She stopped outside Prize's stall, debating whether to enter. Ashleigh could feel the pull of her heart when she looked at the little mare and her new colt. She didn't want to get attached to them. But it wouldn't be right to brush the other horses and not these two.

She opened the door and stepped inside. Morning bobbed his head and took several awkward steps toward Ashleigh, stretching his lips to nibble on her shirt. Ashleigh smiled and lifted her hand to pet him, then stopped midair. She *did not* want to fall in love with this little guy. And Morning was doing his best to convince her otherwise.

Ashleigh picked up the brush box and exited the stall. Caroline could groom these two. It was almost dinnertime, anyway. She had worked the entire day. It was time to take a break. She looked forward to walking into the house and smelling all the good cooking smells of the holiday.

Ashleigh walked slowly up to the house, turning to look at Mona's old farm before she went inside. She sighed. Tomorrow was Thanksgiving, but Ashleigh wasn't sure what all she had to be thankful for. Her best friend was gone, and her favorite horse was living at somebody else's farm. She opened the door, wondering when this empty ache inside her would ever leave.

Later that night, after a big dinner and a sneaked taste of the pumpkin pie, Ashleigh followed her father down to the barn to help check the mares. It was still snowing and blustery. She pulled her jacket tightly about her. When they entered the stable, Jonas was standing in the aisle with a bewildered look on his face.

"What's wrong?" Mr. Griffen asked.

"It's Prize and her colt," Jonas said, pointing at the open stall door. "They're gone."

Ashleigh was stunned. Gone? But she had just visited them a couple of hours ago. She thought back to that visit, and her heart filled with dread. Had she remembered to lock the door?

"Let me take a quick peek around the barn to see if she's hiding somewhere," Mr. Griffen said. "Ashleigh, run up to the house and get your mother. We may have to organize a search party."

Ashleigh sprinted out into the snow. She hoped Special Prize and her colt weren't wandering in this horrible weather. The poor foal was so tiny, he wouldn't survive long. She felt guilty for not checking to make sure she had latched their door.

Ashleigh gathered the rest of her family—all except for Rory, who was already fast asleep in bed. They searched the Edgardale property for an hour before giving up.

Mr. Griffen called everyone into the tack room. "The snow's coming down too fast," he said. "I don't want to endanger anyone. We'll start looking again first thing in the morning."

That night, when Ashleigh closed her eyes, she saw an image of Prize and Morning standing out in the cold snow. She tried to get the pair of horses out of her head, but they wouldn't leave. She knew that if anything happened to them, she'd feel awful!

Ashleigh's eyes flew open wide. Somehow the little gray mare and her colt had wormed their way into her heart. Mona had been right, Ashleigh thought. No matter how hard she tried to avoid it, horses were in her blood. She couldn't help getting involved with them.

The next morning Ashleigh was up at the first light of dawn. She followed her parents out into the cold morning, hoping that by some miracle Prize and her foal would be back at the barn. But the glum look on Jonas's face when they entered the barn told her all she needed to know.

Ashleigh breathed a heavy sigh. She could see the look of concern on the adults' faces. Time was running out for the weakened mare and new foal. They had to find them soon.

"Ashleigh," Mr. Griffen said. "Jonas and I are going to take out the truck and check at some of the nearby farms. I want you to go with your mother to bring Frisky home from the Gardners'."

Ashleigh nodded. It was going to be really weird going to Mona's house and seeing the place empty. She grabbed a halter and lead rope and followed her mother out the door.

When they reached the Gardner place, Ashleigh

looked around, feeling as empty as the old house looked. She put down her head and followed her mother to the barn. She didn't even want to see this place and be reminded of her current loss. Ashleigh decided this was going to be one of her worst holidays ever!

Mrs. Griffen put her arm around Ashleigh's shoulders as they walked. "I know things look bleak, Ashleigh, but it's the holidays, and you still have plenty to be thankful for."

Ashleigh frowned. She couldn't think of anything that had gone right in quite a while.

Frisky whinnied when she heard them approach. Ashleigh's head snapped up when another horse called in answer.

"That extra whinny didn't come from our farm," Mrs. Griffen said in surprise.

They turned the corner, and there, in an old shed, were Surprise and Morning.

"They're here!" Ashleigh cried as she ran to the mare and her colt. "And they're okay. They must have spent the night in here!" She giggled as Morning stepped boldly up to her and nibbled on her jacket.

They heard the old truck as it bumped down the driveway. Mrs. Griffen ran out to flag down her husband. "Grab some extra halters," she said. "We found the runaways, and they're okay."

Ashleigh threw her arms around Prize's neck, giving in to the feeling of caring for another horse. Morning poked her with his muzzle, trying to get some attention for himself. Ashleigh laughed. Maybe her mother was right. She *did* have many things to be thankful for. She had just been too stubborn and selfish to notice.

Several minutes later her father returned with the halters, and they walked Frisky and the new mother and colt back to Edgardale. Ashleigh couldn't help but smile as she led Prize down the road. It was beginning to feel like the holidays!

They settled the horses in at Edgardale and finished their daily chores. Then everyone, including Jonas, went to the house for a big holiday celebration.

The phone rang about an hour before dinner. Mrs. Griffen answered it, listening intently before smiling and hanging up.

"Who was that?" Ashleigh asked.

Mrs. Griffen smiled again as she pulled three more plates from the cupboard and set them on the table. "We're going to have company," she said.

"Who?" Rory said as he looked up from his card game with Caroline and Jonas.

Mrs. Griffen laughed. "It's a special surprise. You'll just have to wait and see."

"Is it Uncle Bill and Aunt Kathy?" Rory asked.

Caroline surveyed the three dinner plates. She

grinned. "I bet it's Aladdin's owners, Mr. Danworth and his family. We haven't seen them in a long time!"

Ashleigh rolled her eyes. "You just want to see their son, Peter." She smiled. "I know who it is. It's our trainer friend Mike Smith, with his family."

Mrs. Griffen listened to the answers and grinned. "You'll all have to wait and see." She looked at the clock. "Our guests will be here in a half hour."

Ashleigh thought she'd go crazy with wondering. They all kept their eyes on the front windows while they played card games to pass the time.

"There's some car lights!" Rory cried excitedly as he threw down his cards and ran to the window.

They all peered into the darkness as a lone car traveled slowly up the driveway. Mrs. Griffen turned on the porch light, and they all went out on the steps to greet the surprise guests.

Ashleigh's heart thumped when the car pulled into the circle of dim light and she recognized a very familiar face. *It couldn't be!*

Ashleigh ran down the steps, sliding in the snow in her haste to get to Mona's car. The side door flew open, and Mona burst from the interior. They laughed as they hugged each other, almost falling down in the snow.

"Why are you here?" Ashleigh cried, then laughed at the way that sounded.

"The house deal fell through at the last minute," Mr. Gardner said. "And since I didn't really like my new job that much, I figured it was a sign that we should stay here in Kentucky."

"You're staying!" Ashleigh squealed.

Mona slapped her a high five. "Best friends for life, Ash!"

"Best friends for life!" Ashleigh agreed.

She locked arms with Mona, and they led the way back into the house, where all the good smells of the holiday season reminded Ashleigh that this was Thanksgiving Day, and she had a lot to be thankful for!